NURSE BOT
CAN SEE
YOU.

Susan Gates was born in Grimsby. Her father is a guitar player and her mother was a tailoress. When she was at school her favourite reading was science fiction and she had a craze for American Literature, especially detective fiction. She went on to study American Literature at Warwick University. She then became a teacher and taught in Malawi, Africa. She has three children and lives in County Durham, England.

SUSAN GATES

SNAIL BOY

AND THE

TOILET BOTS

Illustrated by Tony Blundell

PUFFIN

Published by the Penguin Group
Penguin Books Ltd, 80 Strand, London WC2R 0RL, England
Penguin Group (USA) Inc., 375 Hudson Street, New York, New York 10014, USA
Penguin Group (Canada), 10 Alcorn Avenue, Toronto, Ontario, Canada M4V 3B2
(a division of Pearson Penguin Canada Inc.)
Penguin Ireland, 25 St Stephen's Green, Dublin 2, Ireland (a division of Penguin Books Ltd)
Penguin Group (Australia), 250 Camberwell Road,
Camberwell, Victoria 3124, Australia (a division of Pearson Australia Group Pty Ltd)
Penguin Books India Pvt Ltd, 11 Community Centre,
Panchsheel Park, New Delhi – 110 017, India
Penguin Group (NZ), cnr Airborne and Rosedale Roads, Albany,
Auckland 1310, New Zealand (a division of Pearson New Zealand Ltd)
Penguin Books (South Africa) (Pty) Ltd, 24 Sturdee Avenue,
Rosebank 2196, South Africa

Penguin Books Ltd, Registered Offices: 80 Strand, London WC2R 0RL, England

www.penguin.com

First published 2005
1

Text copyright © Susan Gates, 2005
Illustrations copyright © Tony Blundell, 2005
All rights reserved

The moral right of the author and illustrator has been asserted

Set in 14/16.5 pt Monotype Baskerville
Typeset by Rowland Phototypesetting Ltd, Bury St Edmunds, Suffolk
Made and printed in England by Clays Ltd, St Ives plc

British Library Cataloguing in Publication Data
A CIP catalogue record for this book is available from the British Library

ISBN 0–141–31517–2

Chapter One

Burbling music came from Connor's picture phone. Someone was trying to contact him.

'Who's that?' thought Connor irritably. He didn't have time for text messages now. He was getting ready for school, shoving the packed lunch that Mum had left him into his backpack. And he still had Scooter, Grandad's dog, to take out for a walk.

But his thumb was twitching. He took the phone out of his inside jacket pocket and pressed the button.

'MEDICAL ALERT!' it said on the screen.

'Eh?' thought Connor.

He could just see a bit of the picture, the top of someone's head. It had wispy grey hair.

'Eh?' thought Connor again, even more

bewildered. None of his friends had grey hair.

Then fear twisted in his guts.

'Grandad!' thought Connor.

Grandad had just moved into his new hi-tech bungalow, specially designed for old people. And Connor had suddenly remembered – Nurse Bot, Grandad's new robot carer, could call up your mobile if Grandad needed help. She even had cameras behind her eyes; she could send video pictures. But she would only call relatives in a real emergency. If Grandad fell over, or had a heart attack or something.

'Oh no!' thought Connor. He felt sick and shivery. Hot and cold flushes were already washing over his body.

Frantically, he scrolled down to see the full picture. It was Grandad, sitting in a chair, with his head thrown back and his mouth open. He wasn't moving.

'He looks dead!' thought Connor.

Ever since that last scare, when Grandad had been rushed into hospital with a heart attack, Connor had been haunted by the thought that it would happen again. And that, the next time, the doctors wouldn't be able to save him.

'Call Mum!' thought Connor. Apart from Scooter, Grandad's dog, he was alone in the house. He didn't know what to do. His brain was a whirling panic.

But Mum was driving to work; she wouldn't answer his call. And Dad was at a conference for a week in Birmingham.

'Call 999!' Connor's brain shrieked at him. But Nurse Bot would have already done that. She could link up with phones or computers, even satellites, without lifting a finger. She did it all inside her robot brain.

'Leave your elderly loved one in the care of Nurse Bot,' the publicity brochure for Grandad's new, hi-tech house had said, 'and you need never have a moment's worry.'

But Connor was more than worried. He was frantic.

He hurled his phone on to the kitchen table, forced his weak, rubbery legs to start moving, and raced out of the house. The door clashed shut behind him.

There was only one thing on his mind: 'Get to Grandad's. Now!'

As he ran through the busy streets, his brain seemed to block off all sounds. He didn't hear the traffic roar or the car horns blare. All he could hear was the wheezing of breath in and out of his lungs, and his own thumping heart. And that gibbering, half-crazy voice in his head. 'Don't be dead, Grandad. Please don't be dead.'

Connor left the houses behind, crashed through a wasteland of weeds and bramble bushes. A spiky branch coiled like a snake round his leg. He tore free, ripping his trousers.

There was Grandad's bungalow!

Connor hammered madly on the door. In Grandad's old house you could walk right in – he was always forgetting to lock the door. But Nurse Bot never forgot.

'Come on, Nurse Bot. Come on, Nurse Bot!' raved Connor.

Nurse Bot opened the door. Behind her eyes the cameras whirred and clicked, photographing Connor's face, matching it up with the faces of Grandad's friends and family that she had filed in her memory bank. Nurse Bot never let strangers in.

Connor dashed past her. There was Grandad, in his chair, with his head thrown back and his mouth open, just like the picture on his phone.

'Grandad!' said Connor. He fell to his knees; his legs were so shaky they wouldn't hold him. 'Grandad! You're not dead, are you?' His trembling hand shook Grandad's knee.

Grandad opened one bleary eye. 'Course I'm not dead,' he said. 'I was just having a little snooze. When I'm dead, I'll let you know. OK?'

Chapter Two

Relief hit Connor like a crashing wave. His legs felt even more weak and wobbly. Grandad was alive after all!

'I-I really thought you were dead!' he stammered. 'Nurse Bot sent your picture. You *looked* dead!'

Connor felt angry too, that he'd been given such a dreadful shock. And so early in the morning, when he was hardly awake.

'She's not going to *keep* doing that, is she?' he asked. He couldn't stand it a second time. 'Not every time you fall asleep!'

Grandad glanced nervously towards the door. '*Shhh!*' he warned Connor. Nurse Bot had very acute hearing, as sensitive as a bat. And you couldn't hear her coming. She glided around on silent wheels.

But Grandad could see how upset Connor

was. He tried to comfort him. He patted his grandson's spiky hair. 'I'll make sure it doesn't happen again,' he promised.

It seemed as if he were going to say something else. But Nurse Bot was in the doorway, watching, listening. She was always watching.

Connor was recovering. He'd got back some of his usual bounce. He looked over at Nurse Bot. 'Hey, Nurse Bot,' he greeted her.

He'd thought it was really cool when, two days ago, Grandad had moved into his bungalow with his new robot carer. And Connor's parents had thought it was the perfect solution. Grandad couldn't live on his own any more. He couldn't move around much: he had dodgy hips and knees. Plus he'd recently had a heart scare. So they'd been only too pleased to shift all the responsibility on to Nurse Bot. She would alert them if they were needed. So long as it wasn't when they were in an important meeting.

Grandad had finally agreed. It made sense to move to a bungalow specially designed to meet his needs. And, anyway, he had no other choice.

'No offence, Connor,' he'd said. 'But I couldn't live with your mum and dad – not that they've asked me, mind. But if they *did* ask, I'd have to say no. Because we'd drive each other nuts! And I'm not going into one of those retirement homes. They're full of old people!'

The only problem was Scooter, Grandad's loony, pea-brained red setter. Dogs weren't allowed in Grandad's new home. But reluctantly, he'd let Connor look after her.

'I'll bring Scooter to see you every day,' Connor had promised.

And the amazing thing was, for all this hi-tech care, Grandad's rent was peanuts. That had made the bungalow impossible to resist.

'I can't believe it,' said Grandad. 'It's really cheap. Only ten quid a week!'

But the brochure, pushed through the door of Grandad's old house, had made it clear that Grandad was a sort of guinea pig. That this whole house was an experiment. It read:

There are more old people than ever. How do we care for them? Here at Friendly Domestic Robots our company is trying its best to find the answer! And we have come up with Nurse Bot, a revolutionary new robot. She is a nurse, companion and security guard

*all in one. We are anxious to test her out. So our
company is seeking the right person to move into our
hi-tech old person's bungalow to have their every need
met by our robot servers, especially Nurse Bot.
Are* you *interested?*

'You bet I am!' Grandad had thought, after
the problem of what to do with Scooter had
been solved. He didn't mind being a guinea
pig. It fact, it was all rather exciting, as if he
were some kind of pioneer. It made him feel
needed and useful again.

And the brochure had said something else
too: 'Are *you* the kind of person who values
your independence? We can help you keep it!'

That had finally clinched it for Grandad.
He was a proud man. He hated relying on
other people, having to ask anyone for help.
'This is the place for me,' he'd told Connor,
waving the brochure. 'This means freedom!'

And Connor had been really excited too.
He'd bragged about it to his mates. 'My
Grandad's moving into this new house, with
all these cool robots to look after him. And
there's this extra cool one called Nurse Bot.
She's like Chief Carer, she's in charge . . .'

Connor looked at Nurse Bot as she slid

9

silently into the room. She wasn't what he'd expected. He'd imagined a sleek, silver cyborg like the ones they made in Japan. That looked like shiny metal humans. That could walk and talk and shake your hand.

Parts of Nurse Bot fitted the picture Connor had in his mind. She was made of sleek silver metal. She had metal arms, and sensitive metal fingers that could perform a hundred human tasks.

The brochure read, 'Can't thread a needle? Nurse Bot will do it for you! Can't unscrew that pill-bottle top or bend down to cut your toe nails? Just rely on Nurse Bot!'

There was a computer screen in her chest that reminded Grandad, in giant-sized letters, what he was meant to be doing at every minute of the day. His timetable for the next half an hour was already up there.

8.10 a.m. TAKE YOUR MEDICINE!
8.20 a.m. EAT BREAKFAST!

Nurse Bot's surveillance systems were as good as any military reconnaissance robot's. Her communication links were top-notch – she could get through to Hong Kong by satellite, or plug herself into the Net and order your sausages from Tesco.

But other things about her seemed strangely unsophisticated, even crude. She had no legs, just a long metal skirt. And, instead of having feet, she glided about the bungalow on castors like a motorized wheelie bin.

And her face! It was really peculiar.

She had a silver, steel, skull-shaped head with wobbly swivel eyeballs that seemed to be on springs. Her lips were two red rubber tubes that could purse up like a cat's bottom, or stretch out into long, thin, red tapeworms.

'Nurse Bot's face can mimic twenty-two human emotions!' the brochure had said.

To help her do that she had eyebrows too. They were iron-grey and bushy. They could twitch, go up and down, like baby mice stuck to her forehead. She had a wig perched on top of her head, with grey hair scraped back into a bun. But the hair was so thin and stringy you could see her silver scalp shining through.

When he'd first met her, two days ago, Connor had shivered. He'd thought she looked really creepy. A mixture of Terminator-type robot and ventriloquist's dummy.

'Why did they make her like that?' he'd thought. That wasn't cool at all. As if whoever invented her had run out of money when he got to her face, or just couldn't be bothered to make a decent job of it. But then Connor reminded himself she was just a trial bot. You couldn't expect her to be perfect. They'd improve her as the experiment went on. Make her less weird-looking.

And that was another slightly unsettling thing. Who were 'they'? Who were the people behind this whole set-up? Since he'd moved in, Grandad hadn't seen anyone from Friendly Domestic Robots. All the arrangements had been made with a distant, robot-like voice on a phone. But the company had left an instruction book, as big as a bible, in the bungalow to show Grandad how to work Nurse Bot. And there was a helpline number to call in case there were any hitches.

'Any problems or worries? Need our advice?' the brochure read. 'Help is just a phone call away! Call Dave, our friendly robotics engineer, on *this* number!'

Grandad didn't mind not seeing anyone from Friendly Domestic Robots. It suited him fine, being left alone to get on with it. He hated people fussing over him, and telling him what to do.

Nurse Bot's goggly eyes rotated towards Grandad. Her lips writhed. She opened them. A strange, quacky voice came out. It asked Grandad, 'Are you all right?'

'*Aaargh!*' Connor staggered back, amazed. 'She can talk!'

Grandad was too busy to reply. He struggled up out of his chair, shuffled a few steps.

'You have to move around when she asks you that,' said Grandad. 'If her sensors don't detect movement she thinks you're dead. And she sends pictures to people's phones. Or calls the emergency services.'

Connor was still reeling from his latest discovery. 'She can speak!' he gasped again. 'Make her say something else!'

Grandad hesitated. The truth was, he didn't know how to make Nurse Bot do anything yet. Not until he'd studied the instruction book.

'Say something else, Nurse Bot,' begged Connor.

Nurse Bot's robot brain seemed to understand his command. 'Time for toilet trip,' she yakked. It even came up on her chest computer screen in large flashing red letters.

8.15 a.m. TOILET TRIP

'What?' said Connor. 'I'm eleven years old. I know when to go to the toilet!'

Grandad looked embarrassed. 'It's me she means,' he said.

When he'd studied the instruction book, he'd have to alter that too. He didn't need reminding when to go to the loo.

Something had just struck Connor about Nurse Bot's voice. The voice coming out of her squirmy lips was mechanical, yakky, like the quack of a tin duck. You'd expect a robot to sound like that. But there *was* something very surprising about it.

'She's Scottish,' said Connor.

'Pardon?' said Grandad.

'Nurse Bot's Scottish. Why has she got a Scottish accent?' asked Connor.

Grandad shrugged. 'I don't understand that either.'

Connor shivered. There were so many things about Nurse Bot that just didn't add up. She was beginning to seem rather sinister.

But then Connor forgot all about her. Because, with a *click* and a *whirr*, Robo Dog came into the room.

'Hey!' said Connor, delighted. 'I forgot there were other robots!'

'It said in the brochure,' said Grandad, rather glumly. '"Our Robo Dog will make up for having to leave your own pet behind."'

'Cool!' said Connor. 'What can it do?'

Grandad's old pet, Scooter, couldn't do anything. She was a doggy disaster. She had a tail like a big red feather that swished from side to side and knocked over vases. She pulled on her lead until her eyes nearly popped out. Mum already didn't like her. Scooter left long, red hairs on their new cream carpet. And she had some very disgusting habits, like drinking out of the toilet bowl.

Robo Dog came walking jerkily up to Connor. He didn't look much like a dog, more like a silver box, with a smaller silver box for a head. But at least, unlike Nurse Bot, he had legs. Even if they were stiff and creaky and made of metal.

His little red eyes flashed: once, twice. He yapped, a high-pitched, tinny bark.

Grandad winced. 'I wish he wouldn't do

that,' he said. 'It goes right through me.'

'Sit,' said Connor.

Robo Dog sat.

'Beg,' said Connor.

Robo Dog sat on his back legs and stuck two metal paws up in the air.

'Look at that!' said Connor, amazed. 'He does what you say!' Scooter never, ever did what she was told. And she was too dumb and daffy to learn tricks. 'Robo Dog's much smarter than Scooter,' he said. 'Fetch!'

Robo Dog's little red eyes flashed: once, twice. Then he obediently lurched across the carpet and picked up one of Grandad's slippers in his metal jaw. He laid it down at Grandad's feet.

'How cool is that?' said Connor. 'Scooter would've chewed that slipper to pieces!'

'How is Scooter, by the way?' asked Grandad, wistfully.

Connor didn't tell him that Scooter was already in Mum's bad books. Just this morning she'd said, 'That dog can't stay here. Your grandad's made *no attempt at all* to train her.'

Mum would have loved Robo Dog. He was perfectly obedient. You could bet he didn't drink out of toilet bowls. And he certainly didn't leave hairs all over the carpet.

'Scooter's fine,' lied Connor. 'Mum loves her.'

Robo Dog clunked back into the kitchen on his creaky legs.

Connor looked at his watch. 'Oh no! I'm going to be late for school!'

'Better get going, then,' said Grandad. Did he sound reluctant, as if he didn't want to be left alone?

Connor said, 'You'll be all right, won't you?'

'Course,' said Grandad, trying to sound cheery. 'It's all so different from my old house – all this hi-tech gear. It's bound to take a bit of getting used to.'

'I think it's great!' Connor told him. 'It's the best thing you ever did, moving in here. I love that Robo Dog.' He couldn't wait to get to school and tell all his friends about it. 'See you after school,' he said, dashing to the front door. 'I'll bring Scooter.'

He reached for the handle on the door to open it. There wasn't one.

'I can't get out, Grandad!' he called, into the living room.

'You've got to ask Nurse Bot,' Grandad called back. 'She opens all the doors electronically.' He added, quoting the publicity brochure, '"It's for extra security and peace of mind."'

'Open the front door and let Connor out, Nurse Bot,' Connor heard Grandad say.

Nurse Bot came gliding, like a dustbin on wheels, into the hallway. For the first time, Connor was alone with her. She didn't say anything. Just fixed him with her goggly eyeballs. But, suddenly, her bushy eyebrows scrunched together and became low and glowering. Her rubbery lips pressed into a tight line. What human emotion was she mimicking? It looked very much like hatred.

'*Naa*,' thought Connor. He must be mistaken. Nurse Bot had his face in her memory bank. She knew he was family, not a threat to Grandad.

Nurse Bot pressed her silver palm on to a touch panel beside the door. Instantly, the door opened.

'Catch you later, Nurse Bot,' said Connor.

He barely had time to slip out the door, when it slid shut behind him.

Chapter Three

Connor thought, 'Oh no, I'm late.'

The school yard was eerily quiet and empty. Everyone had already gone into the building. Except for one boy.

He was huddled up against a brick wall. What was he doing? He had a little twig. And he was poking it into a crack in the wall. Now he was pulling the twig out.

As Connor rushed by he saw, or thought he saw, that the twig had a big, grey snail stuck to the end.

Connor shook his head sadly. Every school had its loonies. At least this one wasn't in his class. In fact, Connor couldn't remember ever seeing him before.

The boy didn't see Connor go by. He was lost in a world of his own, concentrating on snail hunting. He stuck his twig into the wall again where clots of snails hibernated, glued together with sticky slime.

He poked about, then pulled the twig out. This time, he'd found a treasure.

'*Wowwww!*' said the boy, his eyes shining.

In the school building behind him bells were shrilling furiously. Ten minutes to the start of school, five minutes . . .

But the boy didn't seem to hear their urgent summons. Or, if he did, he didn't think it was important. He was busy inspecting his prize. The snail was beautiful. Its shell was palest brown, almost translucent, with delicate gold bands going round it. It would be the pride of his collection.

Gently, the boy prised the snail off the twig and put it into his pocket.

The school secretary was looking out of her window. She thought, 'School's started. What's that child doing out there?' She went bustling out to fetch him in.

Connor slipped into his seat, just seconds before his teacher, Mrs Dixon, walked into the classroom. 'That was close,' thought Connor. Now he wouldn't be marked absent. He breathed out a long thankful sigh. He seemed to have been rushing around ever since he got up. He felt wrung out, wrecked. But now lessons had started he could just have a little rest, let himself drift away.

He closed his eyes.

'Connor!'

Connor's eyes shot open. He stared round, bewildered. Had he dozed off? Why was Mrs Dixon yelling his name? She was standing at the front of the class and beside her was . . .

'Snail Boy!' breathed Connor.

'. . . Sleeth is new to this school,' Mrs Dixon was roaring, in her bright, chirpy bellow. 'It's his first day today.'

Connor thought, 'What was his first name?' He hadn't caught it. He'd been too busy staring at the scruffy, hunched figure of Snail Boy. He had his head down. He was shuffling his feet. His whole body was sort of curling up, as if he hated being the centre of attention.

'He's overdone the hair gel a bit,' thought Connor. Snail Boy's tatty hair was stuck into spikes. It glittered, slimily, in the light.

'And as you know,' yelled Mrs Dixon, as if they were all deaf, 'we have a buddy system in this school. Where every new starter is given a friend to help them settle in.'

Why was Mrs Dixon staring straight at Connor? Why was Connor's stomach twisting into knots of apprehension?

'Oh no,' thought Connor. 'Not me, please not me. I've got enough problems already.'

But Snail Boy was already weaving his way towards him through the tables, carrying his chair. There was an ear-splitting squeal of chairs, scraping along the floor. It was other kids budging up to make room so that Snail Boy could sit right beside Connor, his new buddy.

'You'll like Connor!' roared Mrs Dixon so that the whole school could hear. 'He's such a happy, cheerful chappie, aren't you, Connor?'

Connor forced a grim smile, through gritted teeth.

He was seething with resentment inside. 'Actually, I'm quite depressed at the moment, if you must know,' he muttered.

But Mrs Dixon hadn't heard. She was thundering on, 'Connor will look after you!'

Snail Boy moved his chair uncomfortably close, so that their elbows were almost touching. What were those silver trails on his sleeve?

'Give me some space!' hissed Connor.

Snail Boy shifted his chair, about two millimetres.

Connor sighed, a deep heartfelt sigh. He felt really, really sorry for himself. It wasn't fair. All he'd wanted, after this morning's bad start, was a hassle-free day.

He'd been a carefree kid before, with no worries. Innocently breezing through life, having a laugh. But that seemed ages ago; that was the old Connor. This new Connor was loaded down with responsibilities: Grandad and Scooter and now this strange, creepy kid who dug snails out of walls to look after. He sighed again, even more deeply.

'Welcome to the real world, Connor,' he thought.

Chapter Four

Connor led the stampede out of the school gates. At last, the home-time bell had rung and he could get rid of Snail Boy.

All day, Snail Boy had followed him round like his shadow. He hadn't said more than a few words. In fact, had he said anything at all? But every time Connor turned round he was there, lurking, staring at Connor, just staring. What was he thinking? It was impossible to tell. He was so secretive, so mysterious, so odd.

Connor had tried to escape. He'd ducked into the boys' toilets. But when he turned round, Snail Boy was there (*'Aaaargh!'*) gazing at him, like a dumb, faithful hound.

Once, at lunchtime, Connor had shaken him off for a few minutes. Out in the yard, Snail Boy had taken his slimy collection of

snails from his pockets and lined them up, on
a concrete step. There were all sorts of snails
curled into their shells. Some snails were big,
tough bruisers, banded with bright colours.
Some were tiny, fragile, with translucent
shells, like frosted glass. Connor, peering out
from his hiding place behind the wheelie bins,
couldn't help noticing that the boy handled
these delicate snails with special care and
gentleness.

Then one of the big snails had come out of
its shell, its antennae quivering. It had crawled
towards Snail Boy's hand, leaving a glittering
silver trail. Snail Boy had lifted it up, held it
near his face. Connor had seen his lips move.

Could he be *talking* to it?

'For heaven's sake!' Connor had thought,
behind his wheelie bin. Could this kid get any
weirder?

Inside his head, Connor was planning
his evening. Go home, grab some grub, then
take Scooter round to see Grandad. At least
Nurse Bot hadn't sent any more alarming
pictures . . .

He turned round, to give one last wave
to his friends. And bumped into Snail Boy,
who was right on his heels.

25

'Look,' said Connor, trying to be patient. 'School's over.'

Had Snail Boy got the message? Didn't he know that, outside school, school rules didn't apply?

Connor walked a few steps. He could still feel hot breath on his neck. He whipped round.

He was staring right into Snail Boy's eyes. They were dark, deep, unreadable. Except, did they have a tiny twinge of hurt in them, of pain, at being abandoned by his buddy?

'Don't be so soft-hearted!' Connor warned himself. The last thing he wanted was Snail Boy trailing after him everywhere.

'Go home!' said Connor. 'This buddy thing – it doesn't mean we're *real* buddies. It's just something the school dreamt up, to make new kids feel welcome.'

Did Snail Boy understand? If he did, he didn't move. He was still practically treading on Connor's toes.

Connor knew he had to spell it out loud and clear. Snail Boy just wouldn't take the hint.

'We . . . are . . . not . . . buddies,' said Connor, very slowly, as if he were talking to a tiny child. 'I just had to pretend. Right?

Because Mrs Dixon told me to. But we're out of school now. So I don't have to pretend any more. Go home. I don't want you following me. Right? I got things to do.'

Even Snail Boy seemed to have caught on. And, this time, there was no mistaking the pain in his eyes. He turned round, his shoulders hunched, and trudged away. Connor saw that a tiny yellow snail, one of the fragile ones with a shell like frosty glass, had crawled out of Snail Boy's pocket. It was struggling bravely up the back of his jacket, like it was climbing Everest.

'*Awww!*' thought Connor. He could feel himself weakening. He hated being cruel; it made him feel bad.

And Snail Boy seemed so lost and helpless. If anyone needed a buddy, Snail Boy did.

'Come back,' said Connor.

He could have kicked himself. But it was too late now. Instantly Snail Boy came dashing back, his eyes bright, like an eager puppy.

Connor sighed. 'What did you do that for?' he raged at himself inside his head. 'Sometimes you're your own worst enemy!' He could see that the little yellow snail had

27

finished its epic climb. It had reached Snail Boy's head and was sitting snugly in his hair, looking around, as if it were on a mountain summit.

'I'm going home,' explained Connor. 'Then I'm taking Scooter to see Grandad.'

Maybe Snail Boy wouldn't want to come. Maybe he had something better to do.

Fat chance. As soon as Connor started walking, Snail Boy did too, breathing down his neck, dogging his footsteps.

'Look!' Connor whirled round, his eyes flashing fire. 'Will you stop walking behind me like that? It's freaking me out! Walk beside me!'

Snail Boy bustled up beside him. He seemed pleased. As if Connor's invitation showed they were special friends. The little yellow snail on Snail Boy's head had his tiny thread-like antennae out. He was waving them around.

'He looks pleased too,' thought Connor, before he could help it.

'For heaven's sake!' Connor scolded himself, under his breath. Any more of this and he'd be as loopy as Snail Boy. He had to resist it, remember his responsibilities.

'Come on, then, if you're coming,' said Connor brusquely.

He started off again, taking big purposeful strides. Beside him, Snail Boy did the same.

Connor shook his head. He could hardly believe this was happening. 'How did I get lumbered with this nutcase?' he was thinking.

He had a sneaking suspicion that Snail Boy thought of him as his protector, his guide. Even his guardian angel. That made Connor very uneasy. But, he couldn't help it, it gave him a tiny glow of satisfaction too. It felt good, being looked up to.

At home, Connor let himself into the house. Mum wouldn't be back from work until six o'clock.

Scooter bounded round them in giddy circles, making a big fuss, her ferny tail wagging so fast it was just a red blur. Connor didn't have the heart to tell Grandad that Scooter hadn't really been pining for him. Scooter loved Grandad, but she was so soppy and scatterbrained that she loved everyone. Even Snail Boy. She leapt up and tried to lick his face, slobbering all over him.

Connor dragged her off. 'Behave yourself, Scooter!'

But Snail Boy didn't seem to mind. He was already sticky with snail slime. A few smears of dog spit didn't matter.

Connor slapped some peanut butter on two slices of bread. He held one out to Snail Boy. 'Want something to eat?'

Snail Boy reached out to take it. Connor found himself saying, 'Aren't you going to wash your hands first?'

Straightaway, he scolded himself, 'You sound like Nurse Bot.' He'd be telling Snail Boy it was time for a toilet trip next.

If Snail Boy wanted to eat a sandwich after fondling snails, then that was his business.

But an image of Nurse Bot had already crept into Connor's mind – her silver skull-like face, her red rubbery lips, her beetling brows. Those camera eyes that recorded your every move, so you could never have a private moment. The way she'd scowled at him this morning as she'd let him out the door.

Why was he shuddering? 'She's just a machine,' Connor told himself.

And she was supposed to be Grandad's carer.

'Come on,' he said to Snail Boy. 'Let's get to Grandad's. Quick.'

They set out, with Scooter dragging on her lead, panting, her tongue lolling out and eyes bulging. Connor shook his head. She didn't even have the sense not to strangle herself.

'Wait until she meets Robo Dog,' thought Connor. Maybe he'd teach her how to behave.

It felt awkward, walking with Snail Boy. He didn't say a single word. So Connor found himself talking, just to fill the long silences.

'My grandad practically brought me up,' said Connor. 'I stayed with him in the holidays cos Mum and Dad were working. When I was little he met me from school every day. I had my tea round his house. I stayed there till Mum came to get me. Me and Grandad, we're like that.' Connor crossed two fingers, to show how his life and Grandad's were intertwined.

Then he paused. Snail Boy didn't want to know all this. He wasn't interested. He was stroking a big, fat snail in his palm, as if it were a worry bead. He wasn't even listening.

But Connor carried on. Now he'd started he couldn't stop. He'd been aching to say these things ever since Grandad got rushed into hospital. Things he could never say to Mum or Dad.

'I mean,' he spluttered indignantly, 'I was round there much more than Mum and Dad. They hardly came round at all – just to pick me up. And then they just honked the horn and stayed outside in the car.'

Snail Boy seemed to be concentrating on his snail. But his left ear, the one nearest Connor, was twitching. So he was listening after all.

'And, me and Grandad, we cooked together. He showed me how to do spaghetti Bolognese! We watched birds in his garden because he loves trees and birds and nature. We saw a woodpecker once, right there, on his bird table –'

'Snails?' said Snail Boy. It was the first thing Connor had heard him say. 'Does he like snails?'

'Er, yeah, I suppose so,' said Connor. 'He likes all wildlife.'

But Connor was rushing to say something else. Something that had been festering inside him for weeks. Now it spurted out, like an abscess bursting.

'But when Grandad got rushed into

hospital they never told me nothing! Like I had no feelings! Like I had nothing to do with it and didn't know him best of all. I thought he was dying! I said, "Is Grandad going to die?" And they looked at me like I was an idiot. And they said, "Of course not. It was just a scare." But how was I supposed to know that, because they didn't even tell me!'

Connor could hear his voice getting shrill and hysterical. But he just couldn't help himself.

'And when Grandad came out of hospital and they said, "He can't live on his own any more," I said, "I'll look after him. I'll do his shopping." Cos I could have, it wouldn't have been no trouble and he'd been looking after me all that time, since I was little. I mean, I owed him! But they just laughed, as if I wasn't being serious, as if what I'd said was stupid. "He needs proper, professional care," they said.'

And that's how Grandad had ended up with Nurse Bot.

'And now I'm scared all the time that Grandad is *really* going to die . . .'

Connor stopped. Why had he said all that stuff? He felt embarrassed that he'd spilled out his private, personal fears to Snail Boy, who he'd only met this morning and who was a weirdo anyway.

But he couldn't help muttering one last thing, as if he was saying it to himself and he didn't care whether Snail Boy heard or not.

'And it's like, "Oh, nothing upsets Connor, *he's* all right." So I don't say nothing. It's like it's a big secret, how I'm really feeling,' said Connor, bitterly. 'A great big secret that I've got to keep to myself.'

And then Snail Boy surprised Connor. His face suddenly screwed up with passion. He nodded his head in fierce agreement. The little yellow snail nearly got shaken off and smashed on the pavement. Snail Boy knew all about the torment of having to hide your true feelings. He knew all about having to keep secrets. He'd been keeping a secret, a really big important one, for most of his life.

'It's lonely,' said Snail Boy.

'What is?' asked Connor.

'It's lonely having a secret that you can't tell.'

This time, it was Connor's turn to agree.

He knew exactly what Snail Boy meant. Having a secret set you apart. Now he'd shared his, he felt a big relief, a sort of bond with Snail Boy. And he'd thought, a minute ago, that they'd never have a single thing in common.

'Do you mind if I ask you something?' he said to Snail Boy.

Why did Snail Boy look so uncomfortable, so fidgety?

'It's only, why do you collect snails?' asked Connor. 'I mean, you don't have to tell me if you don't want to . . .'

'Oh, that,' said Snail Boy. 'Well, it's because . . . It's because . . .'

Then Snail Boy seemed to close up like a clam. Not another word escaped his lips.

Connor shrugged. He wasn't offended. In fact, he sympathized. Maybe Snail Boy wasn't good with words. Maybe he didn't like talking about his private feelings.

But Connor didn't know the real reason that Snail Boy couldn't trust himself to speak, or to open up to anyone. What if he blurted out the Sleeth family secret? It was a secret he must never, ever tell.

If he did, the consequences would be

terrible. His dad had warned him often enough. Lots of people's lives would be ruined. The lives of strangers and the lives of people he loved, like his dad and sister.

That's why Snail Boy stayed silent. And found consolation in collecting snails. Every snail in his pocket knew his secret. He'd whispered it to them, knowing they could never pass it on.

'There's Grandad's house,' Connor told Snail Boy.

Connor thought it was a weird place to put an old person's bungalow, on a derelict industrial estate. It was so out-of-the-way. No one came here any more, not since the factories and offices had closed. Now nature had taken over, made it into a green wilderness.

Apart from Grandad's bungalow, there was only one other building still standing. It was an ugly warehouse-type building with grey, windowless walls. Connor wondered why it hadn't collapsed. Why it wasn't a pile of rubble, with grass and ivy growing over it, like the other buildings. It even looked as though it was still being used.

But then Connor heard a crow of delight from Snail Boy. He was crouching in some tall purple weeds. This jungly wasteland was a snail hunter's paradise!

He showed his latest find to Connor. It was two tiny orange snails, stuck together.

Alarm bells rang in Connor's brain. But he still asked, 'What are they doing?'

'Making babies,' said Snail Boy.

Then, to Connor's amazement, Snail Boy became really chatty. The subject of snails always loosened his tongue. He could talk about them for ages. And there was no danger of letting slip anything he shouldn't. Snails and the Sleeth family secret were worlds apart.

'One snail, right,' said Snail Boy, waving his arms about excitedly, 'shoots this little rope of slime at the other. Like a sort of lasso. And it ties them together. It's so sweet.' He put the two snails tenderly back on a grass stem. 'Look at them, *awww*, getting all romantic,' cooed Snail Boy.

Connor hadn't really wanted to know about snails' sex lives. But he didn't want to crush Snail Boy's enthusiasm either, not when he'd just got so talkative. So he said, 'You seem like an expert.'

'I am,' said Snail Boy, proudly. 'I've

learned all I know about sex from snails.'
He tiptoed away. '*Shhh*,' he said. 'Let's leave
them. They need some privacy.'

Connor stared after Snail Boy in horror.
It was worse than he thought. Snail Boy
already seemed strange, as if he could never
fit in with normal kids. But how was he
going to survive if all he knew about sex was
from snails? How was he ever going to get a
girlfriend if he thought you had to lasso her
first with slimy ropes?

As his buddy, it was Connor's duty to put
him right, tell him the real facts of life so he
didn't get laughed at.

'But not today,' thought Connor. He just
couldn't face it today. Besides, what kind of
family did Snail Boy come from? Why hadn't
they prepared him for life better? Told him
the things that every boy needs to know?

But the facts of life could wait. There were
more urgent things Connor had to tell Snail
Boy. He hadn't even mentioned Nurse Bot
yet. It could be a bit of a shock, meeting her
for the first time, if you hadn't been warned.

'Wait!' cried Connor, running after Snail
Boy. 'There's something you should know.
My grandad's got this robot carer . . .'

Chapter Five

onnor let Scooter off the lead. Scooter went bounding up to the bungalow. When she saw Grandad staring out of the window, she went wild with excitement.

She raced round in crazy circles, like a red spinning top, barking and chasing her tail.

'Calm down,' said Connor. He'd seen Grandad's face at the window too. He thought it looked tired out and a bit sad.

But when Grandad saw Connor his face lit up. Why didn't he come to the front door to let them in? Then Connor remembered. Nurse Bot locked and unlocked the doors. It was for extra security, Grandad said, and peace of mind. So no strangers got in.

But no one came to answer the door. And Grandad was still staring helplessly out of the window, as if there was nothing he could do about it.

Connor crouched down. He opened the letter box to yell through it. 'Nurse Bot, let us in!'

Perhaps she hadn't seen them. She must be busy, in the kitchen or something, doing little jobs for Grandad.

Connor peered through the letter box, then reeled back. Nurse Bot was there, on the other side, right behind the door. He could see her sensitive, steel fingers, jointed like lobster legs. He could see her hard, shiny, silver skirt.

'Tell her to let us in, Grandad!' yelled Connor through the letter box. Nurse Bot was supposed to obey!

Connor heard Grandad's voice. It sounded weak and faint. It sounded as if he was almost begging. 'Come on, Nurse Bot, open the door. It's not a burglar. It's only Connor. You know him. He's family.'

Connor peered through the letter box again. What was that clicking noise? It was Nurse Bot, tapping her fingers against her steel skirt, as if she were playing for time. She didn't say anything. But Connor could see her computer screen. It had two red words flashing on it. They said, 'GO AWAY!'

Connor rubbed his eyes. They must have been playing tricks. Because when he looked again, the words had vanished. And Nurse Bot was obediently opening the door. She came gliding out into Grandad's tiny front garden.

'Nurse Bot, this is –' began Connor. He'd been about to introduce Snail Boy. Then remembered he still didn't know Snail Boy's first name.

But Snail Boy was staggering back. '*Aaaargh!*'

In an instant, Nurse Bot had changed from carer into fearsome monster. 'INTRUDER! INTRUDER!' flashed up on her computer screen.

Her eyeballs seemed to blaze fire. Her writhing lips stretched into a snarl. 'SSSSS!' she hissed at Snail Boy.

Her fingers clawed into silver talons. She raised them as if she were going to scratch Snail Boy's eyes out.

Scooter ran off, yelping, into the long grass.

Now Nurse Bot's rubber mouth widened into a great gaping hole. Out of it came the most terrible, ear-shattering, wailing sound, like an air-raid siren, while her chest flashed, 'INTRUDER! ALARM! ALARM!'

She rushed towards Snail Boy like a pouncing tiger.

'Run!' Connor yelled at Snail Boy. But Snail Boy was frozen to the spot, too shocked to move. His mouth hung open, his terrified eyes stared up at Nurse Bot.

'Grandad!' yelled Connor. 'Do something!'

Panicky thoughts raced through Connor's head. 'How do I switch her off?' Connor didn't know that he couldn't switch Nurse Bot off. Nor could Grandad. Only the person who'd built and programmed her could do that.

'No, Nurse Bot!' yelled Connor, ramming his hands over his ears as the wailing siren got shrill enough to break glass.

But Nurse Bot was towering over Snail Boy. He was cowering now, his hands over his head. Her face was twisted in hatred. Her claw-like fingers were raised to strike. They glinted in the sun. Showers of blue sparks came crackling out from the ends.

She wasn't going to scratch Snail Boy's eyes out. She had much more hi-tech attack techniques than that. She could make her hands high voltage.

'No, Nurse Bot!' screamed Connor again.

Then Grandad's voice behind Nurse Bot said, 'Friend, Nurse Bot. Friend!'

Nurse Bot didn't obey instantly. 'Friend!' Grandad insisted again.

Then, suddenly, the wailing siren faded away. The claws lowered, the sparks died. 'FRIEND' flashed up on Nurse Bot's computer screen. And Nurse Bot was transformed, from fierce tiger back into carer. Her rubber lips forced themselves into a welcoming smile.

'Come in, friend,' she yakked, in her Scottish accent.

'Grandad!' gasped Connor. 'I didn't know she could attack!'

Even Grandad looked shaken. 'Well, she's a security bot as well as a care bot, you know,' he said. 'She's meant to protect me.'

'But she was going to give my buddy an electric shock. Didn't you see her?'

Grandad tried to shrug off the incident. 'It probably wouldn't have hurt him. Probably just a little warning tingle.'

'Are you kidding, Grandad? She looked like she wanted to fry him to a crisp!'

'Don't be silly,' said Grandad, uneasily. 'She's programmed not to harm humans. Not even intruders.'

But Connor still wasn't reassured. 'But I couldn't make her stop. She was out of control!'

'It's just a question of knowing the right commands,' said Grandad, trying to sound confident. 'She won't do it again. Your mate's face is in her memory bank now, filed under "friend". Tell him to come and meet her.'

But Snail Boy wasn't going to come anywhere near Nurse Bot. He was too traumatized. Gibbering with terror, he went racing off into the bushes.

'Shouldn't you go after him?' asked Grandad.

Connor could see Snail Boy in the distance, squatting in a little clearing. He was already taking his snail collection out of his pocket, arranging them in rows. That would calm him down, better than Connor could.

'Best to leave him on his own for a bit,' said Connor. He was more worried about Grandad than Snail Boy. Grandad looked worn out.

'Are you all right?' Connor asked him.

Grandad winced. Nurse Bot kept asking him that question. Every time he hadn't moved or spoken for five minutes. And he daren't ignore it, in case she sent scary pictures to Connor, or even called out the paramedics. He was exhausted. She was always spying on him; she didn't give him a moment's rest. Her goggly camera eyeballs recorded his every move.

But Grandad didn't tell Connor. He didn't want to worry him. And he wasn't going to tell Connor that he couldn't reprogram Nurse Bot because the instruction book was in Japanese. Or reach Dave, the friendly robotics engineer, on the helpline either. That he just kept getting a recorded message, 'Your call is in a queue.'

Scooter came wriggling on her belly up to Grandad. All the time, she watched Nurse Bot out of the corner of her eyes.

'Hey, girl!' said Grandad, scratching Scooter behind the ears. 'Have you missed me? No need to be scared. It's only a machine.'

'Let's take her in to meet Robo Dog,' said Connor. He was the perfect pet. Maybe he could give Scooter a lesson or two.

Inside the bungalow, there was no sign of Robo Dog. 'Where is he?' asked Connor, disappointed. He searched in all the cupboards. Nurse Bot's eyes swivelled, recording his every move, watching him like a hawk, her lips pressed tightly together like red tapeworms.

'I don't think he's in the house,' said Grandad.

'But where did he go?' asked Connor. 'How did he get out? Did Nurse Bot open the door for him?'

Grandad shrugged. 'I didn't see her.' There were lots of things about his new, hi-tech home he didn't understand. But once he got through to Dave on the helpline all his questions would be answered.

'Some other bots have turned up, though,' said Grandad.

Right on cue, Hoover Bot came gliding from under the sofa like a silver frisbee. It made a low humming sound, like a bee buzzing among flowers. Its sensors stopped it bumping into the furniture. It sucked up dirt while soft brushes underneath cleaned the carpet.

'Cool!' said Connor. 'Scooter should see this. Where is Scooter, by the way?'

'She went into the bathroom,' said Grandad. 'She's probably drinking out of the toilet bowl.'

Suddenly, there was a frantic yelping sound. A red blurry streak came rocketing out of the bathroom and cowered, trembling, behind the sofa.

'Scooter!' said Connor. 'What scared you?'

He went into the bathroom to investigate. Nurse Bot didn't follow him. But her all-seeing eyes swivelled to the right, to keep a check on him.

Connor looked around at the sparkling white tiles, the shower, the bath, the sink. He shrugged. There was nothing scary here. It was just like everyone else's bathroom. So why had Scooter been spooked like that?

'It's just Scooter, being brainless,' Connor told himself.

While he was here, he might as well use the toilet. He turned round. Nurse Bot was spying on him through the open door. She was only a robot, but Connor went to close the door. 'Excuse me, I need some privacy,' he told her.

Nurse Bot couldn't understand those words. She was only programmed to recognize simple human speech like, 'Open the door, Nurse Bot', or 'Make me a cup of tea'. But there was something going on in her robot circuitry. Because, when Connor closed the door, her bushy eyebrows glowered.

'NURSE BOT CAN SEE YOU,' flashed up triumphantly on her computer screen as her robot brain connected up with a video camera hidden behind one of the spotlights on the bathroom ceiling.

Grandad always closed the bathroom door. Like Connor, he didn't realize he could still be watched. It was for his own good. What if he slipped on the tiles and fell over?

'NURSE BOT KNOWS BEST,' came up on the screen as her rubber lips became fat pink slugs and pursed up in what looked very much like a self-satisfied smirk.

Connor went back to the toilet, and lifted the lid.

'*Aaaargh!*' There was something moving about in there!

'Grandad! Grandad!' he yelled. Grandad came shuffling in. 'What's up?'

Connor, his hand shaking, pointed towards the toilet bowl. Grandad peered in, then laughed.

'It's all right. It's only my Toilet Bots. They won't hurt you.'

Connor crept forward. No wonder Scooter had raced out of the bathroom yelping. Tiny bots swarmed in the toilet bowl, swimming in the water like little silver frogs. They were smaller than a five-pence piece. Each one had two blue glowing eyes as big as pinheads, and six slender legs – four with suckers to climb and two with claws to scrape off limescale – and a back end that was a dinky, rotating loo brush.

'They're a bit of a shock at first, aren't they?' Grandad smiled.

Grandad had been shaken himself, on his first toilet trip, when he'd stared down and found dozens of goggly eyes staring back at him.

'What are they doing in your toilet?' asked Connor.

'Keeping it clean,' said Grandad. 'That's their job.'

Now Connor looked closer, he could see the busy little bots, their brushes whirring, cleaning under the rim and scraping away at the sides. And now Grandad came to mention it, his toilet did look sparkling.

'*Awww*, they're cute, aren't they?' said Connor, enchanted by the tiny blue-eyed bots.

Grandad nodded. 'Listen.'

Connor bent his ear close to the toilet bowl. He could hear a sort of twittering from the colony of Toilet Bots, like baby birds in the nest. A sort of chirruping, as if they were singing to each other.

Grandad said, 'I've grown quite fond of them.' When Nurse Bot prodded him awake, yakking, 'Are you all right?' and then quacked, 'Time for toilet trip,' and he stumbled, groggily, into the bathroom, they greeted him with their cheery little toilet-cleaning song. It made them seem really friendly. Much more friendly than Nurse Bot, who was beginning to seem to Grandad more like a prison guard than a carer.

'Are they nanobots?' asked Connor, suddenly worried. 'I read about these teeny-weeny bots that can take over the world. Turn it into grey goo!'

'I told you, they're harmless,' said Grandad. 'They're just domestic bots. All they do is clean your toilet. And when they're resting, they hang upside down under the rim. You can't even see them. They mind their own business as well,' added Grandad, darkly.

'It's a pity Nurse Bot isn't more like them,' he was thinking. She wanted to pry into every aspect of your life, even your personal, private toilet habits.

Reassured, Connor watched the industrious little bots, scurrying about and crawling up the white slippery sides on their sucker feet, like tiny mountaineers. Swimming across the toilet bowl, as if it were a great lagoon. Diving down to the U-bend. All to make Grandad's toilet sparkle. He thought of them hanging under the rim, when they'd finished work, like tiny silver bats.

'I want some!' said Connor. 'For our bathroom. I need never clean the toilet again!'

He never did clean it. His mum did. But that wasn't the point. Toilet Bots were so cute, so cool to have around. His friends would be really jealous.

'What do they run on?' asked Connor eagerly. Could you get batteries that small?

'That's what's so amazing,' answered Grandad. 'I've been watching them, trying to work it out – and I think they're what's called self-energizing. They use the debris they scrape off the toilet sides and convert it into fuel inside them.'

'*Urgh*,' said Connor. That made them a bit less cute.

'So, in fact, they are running on human poo,' explained Grandad helpfully, just in case Connor hadn't understood.

'Yes, yes, Grandad, I get it,' shuddered Connor. 'You don't need to go into details.'

'But it's so energy efficient!' raved Grandad, who, in the short time he'd known them, had become a big fan of Toilet Bots. 'So brilliantly simple! *You* provide fuel for your own Toilet Bots! And it doesn't cost you a penny! How clever is that? Every toilet should have some.'

Connor agreed with that last bit. He'd been beginning to think this hi-tech bungalow was really sinister, with Nurse Bot being so strict and bossy, and watching you every second with her eagle eyes. Then trying to attack your friends. But these Toilet Bots made up for that – almost.

'Friendly Domestic Robots seems to go in for self-energizing bots,' said Grandad. 'There's another one in the back garden.'

'What's that one run on?' asked Connor suspiciously.

'You'll never guess,' said Grandad. 'But come and see for yourself.'

Connor followed Grandad to the back door. Grandad gave Nurse Bot a quick sideways look, as if he expected her to say something. Her eyes swivelled as they passed her. But she didn't try to stop them.

Scooter stayed, shivering, behind the sofa. Having Toilet Bots clinging, like tiny crabs, to her nose was something she didn't want to repeat.

Connor searched for the door handle. Then he remembered. There wasn't one; Nurse Bot opened the doors electronically.

She came gliding up. 'Open the back door, Nurse Bot,' said Grandad.

Nurse Bot's bushy brows scrunched into a stern line. 'Time to take pills,' she said. It was already on Grandad's timetable on her screen:

5.10 p.m. TAKE PILLS!

The letters turned red, then began flashing. Several more exclamation marks appeared.

'I'll do it later,' said Grandad.

Nurse Bot's eyeballs wobbled on their

springs. Her rubber lips stretched, grotesquely, into a gaping 'O' that seemed to take up her whole face.

Connor covered his ears. 'She's going to make that noise again! She's going to give us electric shocks!'

'Of course she isn't!' said Grandad. 'Don't be silly! She only does that to scare intruders. I've told you, she's programmed not to harm humans.' But then he added, looking a bit embarrassed, 'I'd better do what she says, though. Or she'll never shut up about it.' He shuffled off into his bedroom, with Nurse Bot bustling after him.

He was thinking, 'Right after Connor goes, I'm going to try that helpline again. Ask Dave how to reprogram her.' He was a robotics engineer – he'd be bound to know. Maybe he'd even invented Nurse Bot. 'I'm going to tell that Dave,' decided Grandad, 'that I'm sick of being bossed about.'

Connor hopped up and down impatiently, trying to see the other bot out of the kitchen window.

Instead, he saw Snail Boy. He'd come creeping out of some tall yellow daisies back to the bungalow. He must have got over the shock of Nurse Bot mistaking him for an intruder.

Connor waved at him. Snail Boy waved back. Connor wanted to say, 'It's OK. She won't do it again. She knows you're a friend now.' But Snail Boy couldn't hear him through the window. And Nurse Bot wouldn't open the door until Grandad had taken his pills.

Snail Boy didn't seem too worried, though. Sorting out his snail collection had calmed him down, and given him back his confidence. Boldly, he came through the gate into the back garden.

Suddenly, he stopped dead. He seemed to be looking at something behind a bush. What had he spotted?

Connor couldn't see anything. The bush blocked his view. But Snail Boy was still staring. At first, he looked puzzled. Then his eyes widened. And a look of stunned disbelief, then of sheer horror came on to his face. He staggered, as if his legs were too weak to hold him. His hands flew up to his mouth. Then he turned and fled, crashing through the wilderness as if demons were chasing him.

'What's upset him now?' thought Connor.

What had given Snail Boy such a dreadful shock? It wasn't Nurse Bot. She was in the bedroom, supervising Grandad, to make sure he took his pills correctly – two yellow ones and a blue one. Although she only needed one eye for that. Her other eye was keeping Connor under surveillance, through a camera on the kitchen window sill disguised as a potted plant.

Grandad came slowly back into the kitchen, with Nurse Bot gliding behind him. 'Surely she'll open the door now?' thought Grandad. It was fifteen minutes until his next toilet trip.

She did. A breeze blew into the stuffy house, bringing with it the smell of flowers and fresh grass.

But, instead of dashing outside, Connor hesitated. 'What's out there, Grandad?' he asked. It must be something really terrible, to make Snail Boy run away like that.

'It's only a little garden bot,' said Grandad. 'Come and see for yourself.'

They walked outside. And, of course, Nurse Bot came with them, to make sure Grandad behaved himself.

'It was something behind this bush,' said

Connor. He trod cautiously. He could feel his heart fluttering. He'd already seen Nurse Bot's sudden transformation; he knew how scary bots could be.

Then the terrible *something* came trundling out. It was a bot on wheels, about the size of a shoe box. It had two long arms that waved about, with grabbers on the ends. And there was a little sliding door in its back.

Connor laughed out loud in relief. He wondered, 'Why was Snail Boy so freaked out by *that*? It's not even scary.'

'What's it do?' he asked Grandad.

'It's a gardener's dream,' said Grandad. 'I'm not so keen on it, though. I don't like killing things.'

'Killing things?' said Connor. It looked such a harmless little machine. 'What does it kill?'

'Snails,' said Grandad.

'Oh dear,' thought Connor.

'Meet Snail Bot,' said Grandad.

Snail Bot sprang into action. Its long, flexible arms, searching through the grass, had located its prey. Its grabbers seized it. It was a lovely, fat, banded snail, with an amber shell and orange stripes.

'Snail Boy would have loved that,' thought Connor. It would have been the prize of his collection.

But Snail Bot had other ideas. The snail was doomed. It was whisked helplessly through the air by a robot arm. The little door in Snail Bot's back slid open, it dropped the snail in and the door slid shut. There was a whirring noise as, inside Snail Bot, spiked rollers started to turn. Then a crunching, squelching sound that made Connor feel quite queasy.

'No!' thought Connor. No wonder Snail Boy had fled in horror, if he'd heard that.

'It can get through a hundred snails an hour,' said Grandad. 'But here's the clever thing. It makes its own power, like the Toilet Bots. Once it's mashed up the snails, it uses them for fuel.'

Snail Bot went hunting for another victim in the long grass. *Whirr, crunch.* It had found one.

'What a nasty little machine!' cried Connor.

Grandad looked surprised. 'It's very eco-efficient. Except the methane gas it makes pongs like rotten eggs. That's a bit of a disadvantage.'

'*Phew,*' said Connor as Snail Bot blasted out clouds of smelly farts from its back end. 'It stinks.' He wafted the smelly fumes away from his nose.

'Anyway,' said Grandad, 'I didn't think you were such a big fan of snails.'

'I'm not,' said Connor. 'But my buddy is. And now he's really upset. I'd better go after him.' He turned round. 'Come on, Scooter!' he shouted.

'See you, then,' said Grandad, rather wistfully, as Connor and Scooter rushed away.

With a sigh, he turned to face Nurse Bot. 'Time for toilet trip' was already flashing in red on her screen.

'All right, all right,' said Grandad. 'Don't get your knickers in a twist, I'm coming.' And he shuffled inside.

Chapter Six

Snail Boy went crashing through the wilderness. Spiky brambles tore at him, and tall purple weeds tipped their pollen on to his head. It stuck to the snail slime and made his hair sparkle, as if it were sprinkled with gold fairy dust.

He hardly knew where he was going. He was horrified at what he'd just seen. Nurse Bot had scared him silly. But that snail assassin, that murdering machine, had shocked him to the core.

'Snails never did any harm to anyone,' thought Snail Boy, stopping to get his breath back.

But he was angry now, even more with himself than with the machine. He clenched his puny fists tight. 'Why did you run away?' he raged at himself. 'That was really weedy!'

He had to go back, find some way to stop that machine. Destroy it, so that snails could live.

It was all down to him. No one else would do it. Who else cared about snails the way he did? Everyone else, especially gardeners, would be cheering. They'd be queueing up to buy Snail Bots. 'What a great idea! I'll have two!'

'SOS. Save Our Snails,' muttered Snail Boy.

He wasn't scared any more; he was on a mission. Even that mad robot Nurse Bot couldn't put him off. He was burning with a sense of purpose. If snails weren't going to go the way of dodos and dinosaurs, he had to act *now*.

His face grim and determined, he turned back towards Connor's grandad's bungalow.

'Who do they think they are, trying to make snails extinct? God or something?' Snails had a right to live, just as much as fluffy, cute creatures like dormice or red squirrels.

Like Connor, Snail Boy suddenly wondered who *they* were. Who were the makers of that evil machine? Probably the same people who'd made Nurse Bot. *They* had a lot to answer for.

'Right!' said Snail Boy, psyching himself up. 'I'm going back. I'm going to stop that machine somehow. And that Nurse Bot had better not get in my way!'

But then, suddenly, in one of the crumbling car parks, parked among weeds and a tangle of tall white daisies, Snail Boy saw the caravan.

'It can't be, can it?' he whispered.

He'd just felt so strong and bold. So fired up with his plan to Save Our Snails. Now his sense of purpose popped, like a bubble, whisked away into thin air.

He walked shakily towards the caravan. 'Is it really them?' he was asking himself.

The red four-wheel drive wasn't there. But he knew that caravan too well to be mistaken. Those blue-checked curtains that kept nosy parkers from staring in; that dent on the side where Dad had backed it into a wall.

And it wasn't like he hadn't been expecting them. It was his birthday tomorrow. His dad and sister always turned up on his birthday. And part of him longed to see them, even though when they came they always messed things up, throwing his mind and his emotions into chaos.

The concrete in the car park was cracked, like crazy paving, as if there'd been an earthquake. Snail Boy looked around. There wasn't another living soul. No sounds, except a bird twittering and bees humming in the daisies.

He crept towards the caravan.

He called out his sister's name, softly. 'Mustella, Mustella. Are you there? It's only me.'

No one answered.

Snail Boy had a strange kind of family life. His dad and mum had split up years ago and gone their separate ways. He had stayed with Mum, and his older sister, Mustella, had gone with Dad.

Mum had said, 'It's for the best. It's the only way. You've got to forget them.'

Snail Boy sometimes told other kids his dad was dead so he didn't have to discuss it. But he couldn't do what Mum said. He couldn't forget them or pretend that they didn't exist. Besides, they still kept in contact. Even though Mum didn't know about it, they always turned up, out of nowhere, at Christmas and on his birthday. For seven years now, they'd never missed once.

Mum would have had a fit if she knew. She tried to keep things normal for Snail Boy. She didn't want him to be dragged into their world. She wanted him to grow up like other kids.

But Snail Boy could never be like other kids. How could he be when Dad and Mustella were like they were? And when he had to carry the burden of the Sleeth family secret?

Every time Dad and Mustella turned up, Snail Boy felt torn in two. He loved his mum – he didn't like doing things behind her back. But he loved his dad and sister as well.

'Dad! Mustella!' he called again.

Mustella Sleeth slid her head round the caravan door.

Snail Boy said, 'You *are* there! I thought you were, you know, *out* somewhere.'

Mustella said, 'Hello, Simon.' Simon was Snail Boy's first name, the name Connor hadn't heard when Mrs Dixon introduced him.

Simon Sleeth smiled at his sister. 'It's great to see you, sis,' he said.

Mustella Sleeth didn't look much like her brother Simon. He took after his mum. But she was the spitting image of their dad.

She had a small, perfectly round head, like a billiard ball, and sleek, silky, red hair. Her ears were small, tucked in close to her skull. But it was her eyes that fascinated you. They were round, black and glittering. They flickered this way and that, always restless, never still, watching everything with the same alert concentration.

'Where have you been?' asked Simon awkwardly. He hadn't seen Mustella and Dad since Christmas. It took time to get used to them.

'Oh, you know,' said Mustella. 'Just around, travelling. Dad's been getting work on farms, rabbit catching.'

Mustella darted down the caravan steps. Her long, slender neck craned this way and that, snake-like, investigating her surroundings.

'Did you get my messages?' she asked Simon, fixing him with that hypnotic gaze.

Simon shivered slightly, tried to tear his eyes away. Mustella didn't mean letters or phone calls or text messages. She meant *mind* messages. Simon's sister had the power to send pictures into his brain. If she was far away, the pictures were fuzzy and faint. But sometimes they were so vivid it seemed like Mustella was in the next room.

'Yes, and I wish you wouldn't do that,' said Simon. It was like she was trying to coax him over to their side, away from Mum.

'It doesn't work with me,' he added.

Mustella grinned, as if to say, 'Oh yeah?' But, 'Sorry, bro,' she told him. 'I won't do it again. I promise.'

But Simon knew she would. It was no use trying to make Mustella do what you wanted. She didn't go to school. Didn't obey any laws. Not human laws, anyway.

'Where's Dad?' asked Simon.

'Driven to the garage to get some petrol.'

'You're not going away again?' asked Simon, dismayed. 'You're staying for a bit, aren't you?'

'Course we're staying,' said Mustella.

Her head whipped round. Had she seen something? She stuck her whole head into a hole in a rotten tree. Nothing there. She pulled it out again. Then finished what she'd been saying. 'We're staying for your birthday. We've got you a present.'

'Thanks,' said Simon.

It was a rabbit-fur wallet last time. He had

to carry it secretly. If Mum found out, she'd know immediately that he'd been in touch with Dad and Mustella. What would his present be this year? It would be something made out of rabbit. It always was.

Suddenly, a patch of tall white daisies quivered. A red blur came shooting out. It was Scooter, running ahead of Connor. They were looking for Simon.

Scooter leapt up, sloppily licking Simon's face. She started barking, as if to tell Connor, 'I've found him!' Then she saw Mustella. She rushed over to greet her too. Scooter thought all humans wanted to play. But one flash from Mustella's hypnotic eyes made Scooter skid to a halt. Another flash and Scooter was shaking, her long hair rippling like a red cornfield in a wind. She shrank back, whimpering. Even Scooter could tell that Mustella wasn't the playful type.

'Stop it, Mustella,' said Simon sharply. 'Leave the poor dog alone.'

Mustella shrugged. 'Just practising,' she said. She grinned at Simon, showing her sharp white teeth. Scooter, as if released from a spell, fled howling into the bushes. Her day was just getting worse and worse.

'That's my buddy Connor's dog,' said Simon. 'We've just been to his grandad's bungalow and . . .'

He was going to tell Mustella about Nurse Bot going berserk, and the nightmare machine that crunched up snails.

But, as he was speaking, Mustella dashed off. She swooped across the car park in one slinky movement, slithering her head under a sheet of corrugated iron. Simon sighed. Mustella was always doing that: rushing here, darting there, craning her rubbery neck, investigating holes and crevices. She could never stay still. It made it very hard to hold a conversation with her.

Mustella came bouncing back. 'Just toad-stools under there,' she said. 'And this.' She held out a big brown snail.

Simon already had plenty of big brown snails in his collection. They were the commonest type. But he was still touched. 'Thanks, sis!' he said.

But Mustella was off again, investigating something behind the caravan.

Mustella had no time for most people. She thought they were weedy and pathetic because they didn't have her powers. Sometimes,

Simon found it hard to convince himself that she still cared at all about him and Mum. But then she'd surprise him by asking about Mum, saying things like, 'I really miss her.' Or doing something kind and thoughtful, like giving him a snail or a necklace she'd made out of rabbits' vertebrae.

'Snail Boy!' gasped a breathless voice.

It was Connor, bursting out of the wilderness, with Scooter taking cover behind him. Connor came hurrying across the crumbling concrete.

'Snail Boy!' he cried. 'Thank goodness I've found you. I never knew about that Snail Bot, honest. I never knew it even existed. I'm really sorry. I wouldn't have taken you there if I'd known –'

A shrill, fierce voice interrupted him. 'His name's not Snail Boy. It's Simon. Simon Sleeth.'

Connor stumbled to a stop. 'Who said that?' he thought. He just had time to see a weird-looking girl darting out from behind the caravan. She had bright beady eyes and a rubbery swan-like neck. It was twisting this way and that.

And then her eyes connected with his.

They were alien eyes, somehow not human. Connor felt himself being sucked into their depths. Suddenly, a terrible fear paralysed him. Fear of what? Whatever it was, it was coming closer! It made his heart race, and his whole body trembled. But he was helpless to run away. He was trapped! A strong, musty scent filled his nostrils. Then he saw, he saw –

'Mustella!' snapped Simon. 'Behave yourself!'

Simon knew perfectly well what was happening to Connor. His buddy seemed gripped by panic. He was frozen to the spot. Mustella was putting pictures into his head. Not the same kind she sent to her brother, but different, terrifying pictures.

'Mustella!' begged Simon. 'He's my buddy! His name's Connor. Please stop.'

No use trying to force Mustella to do what you wanted. She wasn't scared of anyone or anything. Her kind fought to the death.

But Mustella relented. She must be in a good mood.

She shrugged, turned her eyes away and whisked back into the caravan.

Connor shook his head like a wet dog, and staggered about. 'What happened?' he said groggily. His face was dead white, like bleached bone. He looked wildly around. 'There was someone else here!'

Simon nodded. He tried to keep his voice steady, as if nothing unusual had happened. He couldn't explain. That would mean telling the secret. And, even if he could tell it, how could Connor possibly understand?

'It was my big sister,' he said, 'Mustella. She's gone back in the caravan now.'

'But who? What?' began Connor bewildered. He didn't feel that hot, suffocating panic any more. That certainty that something was coming to get him and that he couldn't escape. The colour was coming back into his face. He couldn't even remember what he'd been scared of. But the ghost of the feeling lingered; his heart was still fluttering, even while the memory was fading away.

'I went a bit dizzy there,' said Connor. 'I felt a bit funny. Your sister . . .'

Simon wanted to comfort his buddy. But he couldn't trust himself to talk. He might give too much away. Connor shouldn't even have *seen* Mustella. That was a big mistake. He knew Connor wouldn't see her again because, out of the corner of his eye, Simon

71

had just caught a flicker in the grass. And he knew the caravan was empty now. Perhaps Mustella was already far away. Perhaps she was up a tree, looking down on them. You never knew with his big sister.

Suddenly, Simon said, 'I'm off home now! See you!'

Connor stared at him.

Simon had been sticking to him like his shadow all day. Connor hadn't been able to get rid of him. But now his buddy was scurrying off, waving, 'Bye!' as if he couldn't wait to get away. Even though he'd found him such a nuisance, Connor felt a bit hurt that Simon didn't seem to need him any more.

'See you tomorrow, at school!' Connor called, before the long grass swallowed Simon Sleeth up.

Then Connor remembered. 'No, you won't see him tomorrow,' he corrected himself. 'It's Saturday tomorrow.'

His mobile rang. It was Mum, back home from work, wondering where he was.

'I'm on my way home,' said Connor. 'I just took Scooter to see Grandad.'

'Is Grandad all right?' asked Mum. 'How's he getting on with his new carer?'

Connor hesitated. In his mind, he saw Nurse Bot with her 'angry' face on. With those red rubber lips clamped together and her bushy brows scrunched into one menacing line. He heard her strict, bossy voice clack, 'Time for toilet trip.'

He didn't want to worry Mum – she was stressed out enough at work.

'Grandad and Nurse Bot are getting on great,' he lied.

Mum said, 'I'm putting a pepperoni pizza in the oven right now.'

That only gave him about twenty minutes to get home. Unless it was the deep crust kind that took longer. Anyway, he didn't have time to hang about.

But, all the same, Connor found himself staring at the caravan.

Simon's creepy sister, Mustella, must still be inside. He hadn't seen her leave. What was she doing in a caravan stuck in the middle of this jungly wasteland? Why hadn't she gone home with Simon?

He shivered, remembering the way her bright beady eyes had seemed to burn into his brain. What had happened after that? He still wasn't sure. Except that he'd been paralysed by panic and knew there was something deadly, stalking him in the dark. And that there was no escape, nothing he could do about it but wait . . .

From somewhere beyond the car park, out in the wilderness that surrounded it, came a thin, high scream.

Connor's head whipped round. The hairs rose on the back of his neck. 'What on earth was that?' he thought.

There were no more shrieks. Only silence. But Connor was trembling now. It was time to get away from this place. Scooter thought so too: she was whining and shaking.

'Come on,' said Connor, putting Scooter back on her lead. 'Let's go home.'

Grandad shuffled into the bathroom and shut the door. It wasn't even time for a toilet trip, but he wanted to get away from Nurse Bot. He hated being fussed over and watched very minute. But it was more than fussing. Nurse Bot was getting very bossy, even threatening, when he didn't instantly obey.

'You're not scared of her, are you?' Grandad asked himself.

He answered his own question. 'No, course

not,' he scoffed. 'She's just a machine. She's supposed to look after you.' And once he'd reached Dave, the friendly robotics engineer, and learned how to reprogram her, he'd be the one in control, not her.

He'd tried the helpline again, just now. But all he got was, 'You are in a queue. Your call will be answered as soon as possible.'

Grandad had slammed the phone down, muttering, 'That Dave must be a very busy bloke.'

Which was strange, because Grandad had thought he was Friendly Domestic Robot's only guinea pig. 'This is our first experimental bungalow,' their brochure had said. 'But we predict it will be a huge success and many more will follow!'

'At least there's some privacy in here,' thought Grandad, leaning against the sink. Away from Nurse Bot's prying eyes. He didn't know that, with her sophisticated surveillance system, she was watching his every move.

'NURSE BOT CAN SEE YOU,' flashed smugly up on her screen as she waited outside the door.

Grandad thought, 'Wonder how my Toilet Bots are doing?'

He limped over to look at them. They goggled up at him with their froggy eyes. They were so cheery, so hard-working, twittering to each other like a cage full of canaries. Some were busy scraping with their tiny crab-like claws; some had their loo-brush tails rotating at high speed.

'*Awwww*,' thought Grandad. You couldn't help being fond of them.

Dear humble little Toilet Bots. They weren't control freaks like Nurse Bot, ordering you about and organizing your life. They just kept themselves to themselves, content to stick to one job – making your toilet sparkle.

'Whoops!'

Grandad had accidentally leaned on the flush button. But even that didn't bother them. They clung to the sides with their little sucker feet while the water swirled around them like a stormy sea. Then, seconds later, they were back at work, scrubbing, scraping and shining.

Were there more of them now? It seemed to Grandad as though his little colony of Toilet Bots was getting bigger.

He was wondering about that when the bathroom door slid open.

'Hey!' said Grandad. He thought he'd locked that. He'd forgotten Nurse Bot had control of every door in the house.

The brochure had said, 'It's so Nurse Bot can rush to your aid if you're taken ill.' It had seemed like a good idea at the time. And Connor had been really keen. 'I won't have to worry about you, Grandad, when I'm at school,' he'd said. 'Nurse Bot will look after you.'

But she wasn't just looking after him. She was taking over his whole life, with her rules and routines and timetables.

'Time for bed,' yakked Nurse Bot. It flashed up on her computer screen in big red letters.

'What?' said Grandad. 'But it's only seven o'clock.'

It was still sunny outside, a beautiful, balmy evening. Grandad thought, 'I don't want to go to bed yet.'

It was time to rebel. Nurse Bot wasn't a carer. She was a tyrant!

'No,' Grandad told Nurse Bot firmly. 'I'm not going to bed now. I go to bed when I like.'

Nurse Bot's lips writhed about. Clamped down on each other. Her face looked like thunder.

But Grandad ignored the warning signs. 'I'm not going to be bossed about by a robot,' he thought. He trudged through into the living room, poured himself a whisky and sat in his armchair. It was very relaxing, watching the trees outside the window, with the birds flickering in them and their lovely misty-green foliage. Sunlight came flooding in and made the room warm and golden.

'This is the life,' said Grandad. He picked up his stereo remote and put on some relaxing jazz music.

'Nurse Bot knows best,' yakked Nurse Bot, gliding into the room.

'So what?' said Grandad. He'd heard all this before. And anyway, what could she do?

'Nurse Bot will get cross.'

'Eh?' thought Grandad. He hadn't heard her say that before. He felt a tiny fluttering in his stomach. Was it fear? He took a big gulp of whisky. That made him feel bolder. Defiantly, he turned up his jazz music to full volume.

'Bedtime,' insisted Nurse Bot. The same words, on her screen, had become giant size. They had four big red exclamation marks after them.

'Get lost, you big metal bully,' growled

Grandad. 'Back off! I'm just sitting here, playing some jazz, having a little drink and enjoying the view from the window.'

There was a rumbling sound. Suddenly, Grandad couldn't see trees or sunlight or birds any more. The room was plunged into darkness.

'Hey!' said Grandad. Nurse Bot had closed the metal security shutters.

The brochure had said, 'All windows and doors are fitted with quick-close, specially strengthened security shutters. They will repel burglars. Even resist a full-scale terrorist attack.'

It had seemed like a good idea, at the time.

His music had stopped too. Grandad fiddled with the remote. Could Nurse Bot control his stereo? Anyway, he couldn't see what he was doing in the dark.

'Switch on the light,' begged Grandad. For Nurse Bot, with her fingertip sensors, controlled the light switches too.

Nurse Bot didn't move to obey.

She glared at him with her goggly eyeballs. Did Grandad see a mean and spiteful glint in her eye? He must have been mistaken. Nurse Bot didn't have emotions.

'Bedtime,' she repeated.

Grandad listened to the silence, stared into the gloom. All he could see were Nurse Bot's eyeballs, glowing eerily, and the flashing instructions on her screen: 'BEDTIME'.

'Actually, I do feel a bit tired,' Grandad decided.

He felt his way to the bedroom. Nurse Bot seemed to have brought all the security shutters down. The bungalow was sealed up tight. Nobody could get in. Or out.

Grandad climbed into bed.

'There's a good boy,' said Nurse Bot. Her rubber lips puffed up into a fat, self-satisfied pout. Nurse Bot had got her way. She always did.

'Night, night,' quacked Nurse Bot.

But she didn't go away. She glided into a corner of the bedroom. Her camera eyes never left the hunched shape, under the duvet. 'NURSE BOT CAN SEE YOU,' flashed up on her screen, just in case Grandad was in any doubt. Nothing escaped Nurse Bot. She had perfect night vision.

Nurse Bot never slept, never went off duty and never ran down. If her stored power supply got low she could plug herself into the mains to recharge herself. She was the perfect carer – or prison guard.

She was silent now. But not for long. Soon it would be time to prod Grandad and ask, 'Are you all right?' And after that, time for a toilet trip. Grandad's night-time timetable was already coming up on her computer screen. He was going to be a very busy bloke.

Grandad wasn't asleep. He lay under his duvet, stiff as a kipper, his eyes wide open and every nerve tense. He knew Nurse Bot was still here. She made a low humming noise all the time, like a PC. It really grated on his nerves. And out of the corner of his eyes, he could see the soft blue glow of her screen. And the twin searchlights of her ever-watchful eyes.

'Leave me alone!' hissed Grandad. But he didn't say it out loud. Nurse Bot might get cross.

And, anyway, he knew it was hopeless. She would never leave him alone, never go away. He felt trapped and helpless. As if Nurse Bot was all-powerful, all-seeing, like God.

'She's just a machine,' Grandad told himself. 'You're supposed to be in charge. You're supposed to be telling *her* what to do.'

Then he thought, 'Better move, or she'll think you're dead.' He stuck his hand out of the duvet and waggled his fingers.

'This is ridiculous,' thought Grandad. 'You can't carry on like this.'

The experiment wasn't working. As soon as he got through to Dave, he'd tell him so.

But he was beginning to lose faith in the friendly robotics engineer. It was taking forever to get through to the helpline. Maybe Dave was just sitting there, with his feet up, having a cup of coffee and ignoring the phone's urgent rings. Maybe he'd even gone on holiday and was sunning himself on a beach somewhere.

'You can't depend on *him*,' decided Grandad. 'You've got to help yourself. You've got to get out of here.' Another day with Nurse Bot would drive him mad.

Grandad lay in the dark, planning his escape.

In the bathroom, the Toilet Bots were taking a break, until Grandad's next visit. They were hanging, like a cluster of tiny silver bats, under the rim, chirping to each other in their own unique Toilet Bot language.

Connor thought they were cute. He'd have been surprised to know that they were the most sophisticated bots in the house. They were much more sophisticated than the crude Hoover Bot or Snail Bot. Even more advanced possibly than Nurse Bot. They were 'self-healing' robots: they could repair themselves. And, like other nanobots, they could self-replicate. With the right materials, such as nickel and titanium, they could make exact copies of themselves. They had been doing that, secretly, for some time.

Even their inventor would have been amazed to know their true talents. Because the Toilet Bots were evolving. Left alone down in toilet world, they were developing their own culture. A growing community of Toilet Bots – a tribe. And, like every tribe, they had dreams for themselves, ambitions. They could plug themselves into a PC, surf the Web. They had been doing that secretly too. They had learned that there was a big wide world out there, beyond Grandad's toilet.

While Grandad lay awake in the dark, plotting his escape from the house, the Toilet Bot tribe were plotting theirs. They weren't, as Grandad presumed, just humble toilet cleaners, content to spend their days making *his* loo sparkle. They had other plans. They would be moving on soon, to bigger and better things.

Chapter Seven

No one got much rest that night. Not Grandad or the Toilet Bots. And, of course, Nurse Bot didn't once close her eyes.

Not far from Grandad's bungalow, the caravan, with the red four-wheel drive parked beside it, still stood in the empty car park. Moonlight filtered through the closed, blue-checked curtains. There was no one inside. Mustella Sleeth and her dad weren't in their beds. They were out somewhere in the dark wilderness, on some mysterious errand of their own.

Simon Sleeth was in bed at home, in his mum's house. But he wasn't asleep.

To outsiders he seemed like an ordinary boy. A bit shy and antisocial maybe, with a strange passion for collecting snails. But lots of kids like collecting things. And Simon lived in a bright, modern, semi-detached, on an estate, like loads of other kids. His mum was a geography teacher. Mum tried to keep their lives as normal as possible. She told Simon, 'You're not like Mustella. You're going to pass your exams, go to university and get a good job.'

Sometimes, they both looked at photos of Mustella and Dad, and had a little weep. And Mum said, 'It's hard, I know. But they've made their choice. They've turned their backs on being human. They won't even *try* to fit in. It was them that split our family up, not us.'

But Simon couldn't pretend they didn't exist. He thought of Dad and Mustella all the time. And he couldn't pretend the Sleeth family didn't have big problems. What other boy had a sister who could squeeze through a wedding ring? Dad's mutant genes hadn't been passed down to him; he'd escaped. But when he was little, he'd longed to be like Mustella. Dad was always telling her, 'You're special. You're a true Sleeth.' And Simon had been jealous of Mustella and Dad's closeness, and of all the attention that Mustella got. He'd felt left out somehow, as if *he* were the weird one, not them.

And what other boy had a sister who could send him mind pictures? Dad was a true Sleeth: he had all their special powers. But even *he* wasn't telepathic.

Dad had told Mustella, 'Be proud. You've got an *extra*-special gift. It only happens in the Sleeth family once in a hundred years.'

That had made Simon feel even more left out and neglected. What had he got to be proud of? He wasn't even a true Sleeth, let alone telepathic. He was just an ordinary, bog-standard boy.

Mum tried to reassure him. 'It's not a gift. It's a curse. You should be glad you're ordinary, and that you're not like them.'

So Simon was stuck in the middle, all mixed up. Sometimes he was on Mum's side. Sometimes on Dad's and Mustella's. But he wished he didn't have to take sides at all.

Mustella was doing it now, up to her old tricks, sending him mind messages. 'You should come with me and Dad, Simon. We have a great time.'

'Go away, Mustella,' said Simon, shaking her voice out of his head.

He knew he was getting himself all upset and confused, just like he always did when he thought about his family situation. Especially when Dad and Mustella turned up. And today was his birthday. He'd just checked his watch. One minute past midnight. He was eleven years old.

He should be celebrating! But first, he needed something to calm him down.

He took some of his snails out of their glass tank. Instantly, his mind was soothed.

Life was so simple, being a snail. And when you got sick of all the turmoil around you, and the difficult decisions, you could just curl up in your shell, and seal yourself inside until it all went away.

He lined up four of his favourite snails on the window sill. They didn't stay put; they went walkabout, leaving silvery trails behind them. 'Come back,' said Simon to a tiny bright-yellow snail. 'You'll fall on the floor. You'll get squashed.'

And then – he couldn't help it – Snail Bot, that murdering, snail-crushing robot came into his mind.

'You know what would be my best birthday present?' Simon Sleeth told his snails. (Apart from his family getting back together, of course.) 'It'd be Snail Bot, in a gift-wrapped box, a heap of mangled metal,' he told them.

Simon was getting upset all over again. That Snail Bot was an abomination.

'Tomorrow,' Simon promised his snails, 'I'm going back to Connor's grandad's place. I'm going to smash that Snail Bot to bits. Then I'm going to find out who made it. And make sure he never, ever makes another one again.'

The restless night wore on.

Connor had managed to doze off. But, even asleep, his brain had been like a giant washing machine, with all his thoughts and worries tangled up together. The scary Mustella Sleeth and Grandad swirled around in it. Toilet Bots had been scrubbing tombstones. A Snail Bot, big as a house, blasting out clouds of eggy fumes and crackling with blue sparks, had chased him home from school, yakking, 'Nurse Bot knows best!'

'No! No!' shrieked Connor as Snail Bot caught him. A robot arm lifted him high into the air. The door in the giant bot's back slid open. He could see those spiky rollers grinding right beneath him –

'*Aaaargh!*' Connor woke up with a start. He was in a sweaty panic, his eyes staring around wildly. Then he saw Scooter was twitching at the end of his bed, lost in her own doggy dreams.

'Calm down, calm down,' Connor told himself. The frightful monster Snail Bot that hunted humans was just a nightmare.

He tickled Scooter's nose until she sneezed and woke up. He wanted someone to talk to about what was happening at Grandad's.

He'd tried Mum. But she didn't want to listen. She'd said, 'Look, he'll have to make the best of it. He's sold his old house now. There's no going back.'

The blackness in his bedroom was fading to fuzzy greyness. It was getting light. Connor made a decision.

'It's only early,' he told Scooter. 'But I'm going to see Grandad. I'm going to rescue him from that Nurse Bot. You coming?'

Scooter's feathery tail swished. A stack of Connor's computer games clattered to the floor.

'*Shhhh!*' said Connor. 'We've got to sneak out, so Mum can't hear us.'

Holding Scooter firmly by her collar, he crept downstairs.

Chapter Eight

In the grey early morning light, Grandad dragged himself wearily out of bed. Toilet trips and Nurse Bot prodding and poking him all night to make sure he wasn't dead had all taken their toll. He'd meant to plan his escape, but his brain felt like sludgy porridge. He ached all over. He felt about a thousand years old.

This was his sixth toilet trip. The Toilet Bots, twittering to each other, zipping round his toilet like busy little bees, cheered him up a bit.

He thought, 'No point in going back to bed. I think I'll go out in the back garden.' It would be beautiful out there: the dewy grass smelling fresh and green, and the spiders' webs sparkling.

Grandad went into the kitchen. Nurse Bot had already lifted the security shutters on the windows. All he had to do was ask her to open the back door.

'Open the back door, Nurse Bot,' said Grandad.

He wasn't even thinking of running away. He couldn't shuffle more than a few steps this morning. His bad knee was really playing up. He just wanted some fresh air – to see birds and trees and flowers.

But Nurse Bot's lips pressed into a thin, disapproving line. Her brows scrunched up.

'7 a.m. GET UP' was highlighted on her screen.

It was only 6.45.

'Back to bed,' yakked Nurse Bot.

Somewhere inside Grandad a rebellious spark still flickered. It was just a tiny feeble light. But Nurse Bot hadn't extinguished it altogether.

'I don't want to go back to bed!' said Grandad. 'I want to go out into the back garden. Now open that door!'

'No,' said Nurse Bot.

Grandad could hear the desperation in his voice. He sounded like a pleading child.

'Please,' he said. 'I just want some freedom. I just want to smell the flowers.'

'Back to bed,' said Nurse Bot, scowling.

'OPEN – THAT – DOOR!' shrieked Grandad. 'I can't stand it in here a second longer. I've got to get out!'

'Nurse Bot will get cross,' said Nurse Bot smugly.

'For pity's sake,' howled Grandad. 'Stop treating me like a child!'

Then Grandad, like a caged animal in a zoo, went a little bit crazy. He couldn't get out of the doors. So he picked up a chair, lifted it and brought it crashing down on the window glass.

Boing! It bounced off, and sent him staggering backwards. He'd forgotten. All the windows of the bungalow were shatterproof glass.

'Even a high-velocity rifle bullet can't break them,' the brochure had said.

It had seemed like a good idea, at the time.

Grandad limped back into the living room, slumped down into his chair. He grabbed the phone. He'd given up on Dave the friendly robotics engineer. It seemed Dave didn't *want* to be contacted. Instead he was going to call Connor, Connor's mum, the emergency services, anyone who'd listen, and yell, 'Come and rescue me from this mad robot!'

But there was no dial tone. Just dead silence. Nurse Bot had somehow sabotaged the phone line. Grandad had no mobile. He'd never used one. They were too fiddly for his stiff, arthritic fingers.

With growing horror, Grandad realized, 'She's cutting off all communications. Isolating me from the outside world.'

There was one chance. Soon Connor would be coming with Scooter. Grandad scrabbled on the table beside his chair for a pen. Paper – he needed paper! He ripped off the back cover of the useless instruction book and scrawled 'SAVE ME' on it in big, black letters.

Nurse Bot didn't try to stop him. But her eyeballs swivelled on their springs, watching every move he made. Grandad heaved himself out of the chair, found a roll of sticky tape in a drawer. Then shuffled over to the living-room window.

The sun was coming up. The front garden was flooded with gentle golden light. Grandad ached to be out there, smelling the flowers, walking in dewy grass.

He threw a nervous glance over his shoulder at Nurse Bot. Surely she wouldn't allow this? 'NURSE BOT WILL GET CROSS' was still glowing in crimson letters on her chest computer screen, like a silent threat.

But she didn't do anything. She just stood there, watching him, clicking her talons against her steel skirt.

With hope fluttering inside him, Grandad taped up his plea for help. He knew Connor would see it and take some action. Connor would save him.

But just as he'd bitten off his last piece of tape, he heard a rumbling sound.

'No!' said Grandad. 'No!'

Nurse Bot was closing the security shutters, so no one could see his plea for help.

'Don't close the shutters,' begged Grandad. 'I want to see outside.'

He stared out as the grey metal shutters came rolling down, cutting off the view. They sliced off the sun's golden fingers, which were just trembling on the window sill. Then, *clunk*, they settled into place.

It was the last straw. Grandad slumped down in his chair in the dark room. He felt like bursting into tears.

There was just one last tiny hope. He took the TV remote and tried to switch on the news. At least he'd feel that there was still a world out there. He pressed the ON button. The screen stayed blank. Nurse Bot had cut off the power.

Grandad let his head fall into his hands. He was sick of the struggle. Too tired to fight any more. It was much easier to obey. Maybe, if he did, if Nurse Bot was pleased with him, she'd stop her spiteful punishments. She might even let him watch telly.

'Back to bed,' yakked Nurse Bot, even though it was 6.55 and in five minutes she'd be nagging him to get up again.

Grandad hauled himself out of the chair. He turned towards the bedroom. His eyes were dull, glazed over, his walk mechanical. He looked more like a robot than Nurse Bot.

Nurse Bot glided behind him so close that, if she were human, her breath would have been hot on Grandad's neck. 'Good boy,' she said as Grandad climbed into bed. She had her smug face on. She knew Grandad was ground down, defeated, and that she'd won.

A line of tiny words came trickling on to her computer screen. They said: 'IT'S FOR YOUR OWN GOOD.'

Grandad lay in bed. His eyes looked empty. There were no thoughts in his head. He was just waiting for Nurse Bot to tell him what to do next.

'Are you all right?' asked Nurse Bot, leaning over him, her goggly eyes gazing right into his. Feebly, Grandad flapped his hand.

Then there was a little flicker, somewhere in Grandad's brain. Perhaps, perhaps, there *was* someone out there listening. *Someone* must be out there, controlling Nurse Bot, looking right now at the pictures she was taking with her camera eyes. Could it be Dave, the friendly robotics engineer?

'Are you listening, Dave?' asked Grandad, raising his head from the pillow and talking not to Nurse Bot but to her goggling eyeballs. 'Is that you? Can you see me, Dave? If you can, please get in contact.'

It was no use. There was no one out there. Grandad felt he was entirely alone, at Nurse Bot's mercy. His head flopped back on to the pillow. He closed his eyes.

*

Grandad didn't know it, but there *was* someone out there, listening. And he wasn't far away. He was sitting surrounded by computer screens. Pictures and sound from the bungalow were being relayed to him by Nurse Bot twenty-four hours a day. He'd invented Nurse Bot and all the other bots. He'd masterminded this whole set-up. But he wasn't called Dave – his name was Dr Charles Darlick.

Dave didn't exist. He'd been invented too, by Dr Darlick, to give his experiment a friendly and caring face. To hide its true, sinister purpose.

Friendly Domestic Robots did exist. It was an above-board, legally registered company. But even that wasn't what it seemed. It didn't have 'a team of top robotics experts' like it said in the brochure. It only had Dr Darlick. Friendly Domestic Robots was strictly a one-man operation.

'That Nurse Bot – she's a tyrant, a fiend, a monster!' moaned Grandad in a feverish doze.

'No, she isn't,' snapped Dr Darlick, knowing that he could see and hear Grandad but Grandad couldn't see or hear him. 'You just don't know what's best for you, that's all.'

'Your experiment's going wrong, Dave,' groaned Grandad deliriously.

'No, it isn't.' Dr Darlick pursed his lips into a smug pout. 'It's going even better than I expected.'

And this was just the start. Dr Darlick had much bigger ambitions than one Nurse Bot, controlling one old person, in one bungalow. He wanted to make the world a better place.

Nurse Bot's inventor got up from his computer screen. He didn't have to check on Grandad and Nurse Bot every second, not any more. Grandad had finally learned that Nurse Bot knew best.

Dr Darlick's eyes strayed to a photo on the wall. Instantly, he stopped slouching and stood up, ramrod straight.

It was a faded photo of his old Scottish nanny, Nanny McFiggins. She had cared for him, many years ago, when he was a boy. But Dr Darlick still worshipped her memory.

He could still hear her stern, Scottish voice in his head. 'Nanny knows best!' He still behaved as if she were watching him, every second, so great had been her influence on him.

Dr Darlick took his hands out of his

pockets. 'Sorry, Nanny,' he mumbled, like a naughty schoolboy. Nanny had hated slouching and hands in pockets, or slackness of any kind. She'd run his life with military discipline.

'There is a wild creature inside every child,' she'd say as she scrubbed his face with a flannel that felt like sandpaper, 'that must be *crushed.*'

Nanny was very keen on crushing people. Not just children. She thought *everyone*, of any age, would benefit from Nanny's strict regime. It was never too late to learn what was good for you.

The photo of Nanny McFiggins showed a severe, unsmiling woman, with hair scraped back into a bun. Her bulging, froggy eyes seemed to follow you round the room, watching your every move. And underneath the photo was written, 'Nanny McFiggins can see you.'

Nanny McFiggins had bushy grey eyebrows and goggly eyes. She bore a striking resemblance to Nurse Bot. Those thin lips, like two stretched tapeworms, that could smile or tighten in anger; the silent way she snuck up on you . . .

In fact, when Dr Darlick had invented Nurse Bot, Nanny McFiggins had been his main inspiration. Just like Nanny, Nurse Bot liked rules and routines. Like Nanny, she punished the slightest disobedience.

He'd even programmed Nurse Bot with Nanny's Scottish accent and some of her little sayings:

'Nanny can see you.'

'Nanny knows best.'

'It's for your own good.'

And the one that still made Dr Darlick tremble. 'Nanny will get cross.'

Reverently, Dr Darlick lifted a little book from his computer desk. It was covered with ghastly red and green cloth – the McFiggins tartan. And the title was *The Wisdom of Nanny McFiggins*. He'd had it printed at his own expense. It was his bible. He read it every day.

Dr Darlick turned to another of Nanny McFiggins's sayings. She used to mutter it every morning as she tugged a wire comb through his hair: '*If there were a Nanny McFiggins in every home, this world would be a better place.*'

Dr Darlick agreed with that, as he agreed with everything that Nanny McFiggins had taught him. Because, if he didn't, she used to shut him in the coal-hole.

'Nanny knows best,' she would say as she shoved him down into the darkness and slid the manhole cover back into place.

'And, of course,' thought Dr Darlick, closing the book, 'Nanny McFiggins *did* know best. I owe everything to her. She made me what I am today!'

'Are you pleased with me, Nanny?' Dr Darlick asked Nanny McFiggins's photo, nervously.

All his life Dr Darlick had been trying to please his old nanny. She'd been dead and buried for years but her power over him hadn't diminished. 'Are you pleased?' Dr Darlick begged her photo, sounding like a small, frightened child. 'Your spirit lives on in Nurse Bot, Nanny! Through Nurse Bot you can make the world a better place! And you always wanted to do that, didn't you, Nanny?'

Did Nanny's stern brows, in the photo, unbend just a little? Did her lips curve up, ever so slightly? Dr Darlick imagined they did.

'Oh, thank you, Nanny, thank you,' he said. He clasped his hands together with joy. He almost fell to his knees, he was so pathetically grateful.

Dr Darlick had dedicated his life to winning Nanny's approval. It was the reason he'd gone into robotics and set up this experiment, spending a great deal of his inheritance.

But one tiny, grudging smile from Nanny made it all worthwhile.

He went off, humming happily, to his tiny cubbyhole kitchen, to make himself a tuna sandwich for lunch.

Chapter Nine

Grandad hadn't been completely abandoned. His faithful grandson, Connor, was outside the bungalow. He'd arrived just in time to see Grandad's sign, 'SAVE ME'. Then the shutters had come rumbling down. Connor's last glimpse had been of Grandad's bleak, hopeless face, staring out like a prisoner who's seeing his last few moments of the outside world, before he's locked up, forever.

'Grandad!' yelled Connor.

But with a *clunk* the security shutters dropped into place. The door and all the windows were covered in cold, grey metal.

'You've got to *do* something!' Connor told himself.

He went rushing up to the front door, with Scooter at his heels.

'Nurse Bot! Nurse Bot!' he yelled. He knew only she could open the doors.

What was going on in there? He couldn't let himself think about that either – Grandad locked in the dark with that metal tyrant, her quacky Scottish voice, her weird bristly brows and those sinister warnings flashing up on her screen: 'NURSE BOT CAN SEE YOU.'

'Open the door, you big bully!' shrieked Connor frantically. 'You freak on wheels! Let my grandad go!'

Scooter, caught up in the general excitement, barked wildly and ran in circles.

'Shhhh, Scooter,' said Connor. He needed to think.

He knew he couldn't batter the door down. The house was armoured, like a tank, fortified as if it was under siege. But still he raised his fist to pound on the shutter.

'Open this door, you metal monster!' he screamed. 'I know you're listening in there.' She was probably standing just behind the door, twiddling her steel fingers and smirking.

'*Owwww!*'

Connor staggered back, nursing his

stinging hand. The shock tingled, all the way up his arm.

'I can't believe this!' he shouted at Scooter. 'She's electrified the security shutters!'

Nurse Bot wasn't going to give up Grandad without a fight. She wasn't even letting his own family near him now.

'*Owww,*' said Connor again softly, shaking his hand.

It hadn't been a very big shock, like brushing up against an electrified cattle fence. But Connor had seen that streak of cruelty in Nurse Bot. He'd seen her turn from care bot to warrior bot in about two seconds. Seen that simpering smile become a vicious snarl. He knew what she was capable of.

'That stuff about not harming humans is a load of rubbish,' thought Connor. He wouldn't trust her not to increase the voltage and fry him to a crisp. He didn't touch the shutters again.

'I want to see my grandad!' yelled Connor desperately. 'Is he all right? It's me, Connor! Let me in!'

But he knew she wouldn't. What was going on in her robot brain? Did she think she was protecting Grandad? Did she want to have absolute control over his life, with no one else interfering? Or maybe she was just malfunctioning, mistaking friends for intruders? That was an even more terrible thought. Grandad, locked up with a mad robot!

'I need some help,' thought Connor. 'I can't handle this alone.'

Who was he going to call? Mum would be at the gym; she'd have her phone switched off while she was working out. But maybe she'd finished by now. It was worth a try.

He reached in his pocket for his mobile. But he'd come rushing out of the house so fast this morning that he'd left it by his bed.

'You idiot!' Connor raged at himself. 'What are you going to do now?'

He paced round the sealed-up house, keeping well clear of the metal shutters. But there was no way in. It seemed impregnable. Then, in Grandad's back garden, he saw a familiar figure.

'Snail Boy! I mean, Simon!' yelled Connor.

Simon was searching in the grass.

Connor sighed. Simon wasn't going to be much help. Hadn't he seen the shutters coming down? That look of hopelessness on Grandad's face? Didn't he care? How could he be calmly searching for snails at a time like this?

But then Simon lifted his head. And his face wasn't calm. It was twisted with such hatred that Connor was startled. He didn't think his shy, snail-collecting buddy was capable of such fierce and intense emotion. It was almost scary.

'Is he angry with *me*?' Connor thought.

But then everything was explained.

'I'm looking for that evil, snail-munching machine,' said Simon, spitting out the words.

'What? Snail Bot?' said Connor. He couldn't get worked up about Snail Bot. Not now. What did a few dead snails matter? When Grandad was being kept prisoner by his control-freak carer?

'Yeah, and I'm going to smash it to bits,' said Simon, scowling. His puny fists bunched up until the knuckles were bone-white. 'Then I'm going to find out who invented it. And make sure he never makes another one.'

'Who invented it?' repeated Connor, looking confused.

'Yeah,' said Simon. He swept his hand over the silent, shut-up bungalow behind them. 'Someone, someone *human*, must be behind all this. Controlling the machines. Telling Nurse Bot what to do.'

'Telling Nurse Bot what to do?' said Connor in an even more bewildered voice. '*Nobody* tells Nurse Bot what to do.'

But then his head suddenly cleared. 'You're right!' he said.

Nurse Bot couldn't be in charge; she was just a robot. Someone must have built and programmed her. Somewhere behind all this, like Simon said, there must be a human brain.

'You're right, buddy,' Connor said again excitedly. 'Grandad had this brochure that explained all about the bungalow. This company called Friendly Domestic Robots set it all up. They're the ones responsible. And they've got a helpline – I remember Grandad telling me.'

'What's the number?' asked Simon eagerly. 'We've got to call them, make them shut all these bots down.'

Connor's face clouded over. 'I don't know,' he said. 'The brochure's back there, in the bungalow.'

'Oh,' said Simon.

They looked at each other in despair.

'So what are we going to do now?' asked Connor.

But Simon was staring at the house. 'Nurse Bot hasn't closed off that ventilation grille.'

'What?' said Connor.

He followed Simon's pointing finger. There was a tiny metal grille, in the brickwork, just under the roof.

'So?' said Connor.

'Someone could get through it,' said Simon.

Connor looked at him, exasperated. You never knew where you were with Simon. First he said something sensible, like there must be a human brain behind all this. Then he said something really, really stupid.

'Who do you know who could get through there?' asked Connor. 'I couldn't. You couldn't.'

'My sister Mustella could,' said Simon.

As soon as the words were out, Simon could have bitten off his tongue. What on earth had he said that for? He'd got carried away, desperate to help his buddy Connor and to do something about that dreadful Snail Bot.

Perhaps Connor hadn't heard?

Fat chance.

'What are you *talking* about, Mustella

could?' demanded Connor, angry and confused. 'I don't understand.'

Straightaway, Simon tried to take back what he'd said, to repair the damage. In all his life, he'd never let slip the slightest hint about the Sleeth family secret. Not to anyone. But now he'd blundered, big time.

'Did I say *Mustella*? I must have been mad. I meant to say,' Simon cast his eyes wildly round, saw the silvery trails on his sleeve, 'a *snail* could squeeze through there.'

'A snail!' roared Connor getting more and more angry and exasperated. 'And what's that supposed to do? Fight Nurse Bot all on its own? Rescue Grandad? Get real!'

Connor's hands crept towards his head. He felt like tearing his hair out. This was an emergency. Anything could be happening in there. Grandad was at the mercy of Nurse Bot. He might need medical attention! Connor had to get to him. But all he had to help him was a pea-brained hound who ran round in circles and a poor, demented boy who thought his snails were superheroes.

'Shhhh!' said Simon suddenly. He clutched Connor's sleeve. 'Something's happening. Look!'

In the shutter that covered the back door, a tiny door slid open. It was no bigger than a cat flap. But it wasn't a cat that came trundling out. It was Snail Bot, puffing out clouds of putrid air.

'You fiend!'

With a fearsome war cry, Simon hurled himself at the smelly little garden bot. He was thinking of all the beautiful snails it had mashed up. He was hungry for revenge.

'You're gonna *die*!' shrieked Simon.

'No!' Connor held him back.

Simon was Twiglet-thin and small for his age but his anger gave him alarming strength. He fought and kicked as Connor struggled to keep him from attacking Snail Bot.

'Let – me – go!' howled Simon, his face bright red with fury. 'It's getting away!'

'It's broken!' said Connor. 'Calm down. Just *look*, will you?'

Simon stopped struggling and looked at the machine. One of Snail Bot's grabber arms was dangling uselessly, trailing along beside it like a bird's broken wing.

'How'd it do that?' said Simon. For one mad moment he thought snails had been fighting back, until Connor said, 'Must have hit a rock or something. Anyhow, it's busted.'

And, instead of starting on another snail-killing spree, the damaged bot was going somewhere else, speeding along the path.

'Where's it going?' asked Simon.

'That's what I was trying to tell you,' said Connor. 'We should follow it.'

Finally, Simon had caught on. The red mists were fading from his mind. He was thinking clearly now. 'Think it's going to be repaired?'

Connor nodded. 'That's what I was wondering.'

'And, if we follow it, we'll find whoever made it?' asked Simon excitedly.

Connor said, 'I don't know.' But it was worth trying. *Someone* was behind all these bots: Nurse Bot, Snail Bot and the others. Someone had masterminded this whole set-up.

Simon was already dashing off, following Snail Bot into the weedy wasteland outside Grandad's garden gate.

'Wait for me!' cried Connor. Already, he'd lost sight of Simon. The long grass had swallowed him up. But a voice came floating back to him.

'It's my birthday today.'

'*Birthday?* What's he telling me that for?' thought Connor, bewildered. 'What's that got to do with anything?' In the present circumstances, birthday celebrations were the last thing on his mind.

But he still found himself calling back, 'Happy Birthday, buddy!' as he plunged into the wilderness after Simon.

Chapter Ten

In the caravan, Mustella Sleeth was having a blazing row with her dad. Except Mustella was doing most of the shouting and Mr Sleeth, a shy, secretive man of few words, was doing most of the listening.

'I'm proud of what I am!' Mustella was yelling.

'*Shhh!*' said Mr Sleeth, darting over to the caravan windows, his snaky neck craning this way, that. 'Someone might be listening.' Sleeths like he and Mustella, who'd inherited the family's mutant genes, always had to be on their guard.

'I don't care,' said Mustella, her eyes glittering like deep, sparkling pools. 'Why have we got to hide away, pretend that we're one hundred per cent human? I hate humans anyway.'

'*Shhh*,' said Mr Sleeth soothingly. They'd had this conversation a hundred times before. 'You don't hate all humans. What about Simon and Mum?'

'I like Simon,' admitted Mustella. 'He's cool.' But she was in two minds about Mum. Sometimes she really missed her. Even cried for her. But Mum had tried to get her and Dad to deny their true natures. Mustella wasn't ready yet to forgive her for that.

'People are just pathetic!' fumed Mustella.

'We've got to learn to live with them,' said Mr Sleeth in his quiet, reasonable way.

'Why?' demanded Mustella wildly. 'We're just fine as we are. We don't need them.'

Mr Sleeth sighed. It was no use arguing with Mustella when she was like this. She wouldn't listen. But he didn't blame her. She was only thirteen. Being a teenager was hard enough anyway. But being a teenager and a true Sleeth, having to keep your real self a secret, was a thousand times harder. He could understand why she often got frustrated, why she ranted and raved.

'I have to go out,' said Mr Sleeth. 'I've got a rabbit-catching job. Want to come with me?

Just don't be rude to the farmer, that's all.'

But Mustella didn't feel like being polite to humans. 'People are pathetic!' she spat out again, and flung herself on to the tiny sofa. And yet they thought they were so great! She'd seen that boy Connor staring at her, probably feeling sorry for her, thinking, 'What a weird-looking girl.' He'd have been amazed to know that she was feeling sorry for *him*, for being a weak and puny human.

'If only he knew our secret,' she thought, grinning. 'Just imagine his face!'

Mr Sleeth didn't want to leave his daughter alone. He wasn't worried that she wouldn't be safe. Since she was twelve weeks old Mustella had been able to take care of herself. But he feared that, in this mood, she might do something silly. Something that would betray the Sleeth family secret to the world.

But he had to earn a living. He whisked out of the caravan doorway. Then stuck his sleek, seal-like head back in. He gave her one warning. 'Just remember,' he said. 'The consequences will be terrible.'

'I know, I know,' said Mustella Sleeth sulkily. 'You've told me a million times.'

'And when Simon comes,' said Mr Sleeth,

'give him this present and tell him "Happy Birthday". Say I'll see him later.'

Mustella put Simon's present on a shelf. Inside the cheery paper, with bright balloons and HAPPY BIRTHDAYs all over it, was a beautiful flute that Dad had made out of the thigh bone of a rabbit.

Mustella slumped back on the sofa. It smelt a bit, of old blood and rank rabbit fur. The whole of the caravan smelt the same. It was lined with rabbit fur – on the walls, the floor, even the ceiling. It made a lovely, cosy den to sleep in.

But Mustella didn't feel like sleeping, or hunting for food either. She didn't know what to do with herself. She was in such a strange, restless mood this morning.

Should she send some mind pictures to Simon? Put some excitement into his boring *normal* life? But she couldn't be bothered to do that either. Her round eyes glittered dangerously. She felt like being really reckless. She was sick of being secretive, hiding away.

'I just want to be myself,' she said stubbornly. 'That's not too much to ask, is it?'

But, if you were a true Sleeth, it was like asking for the moon.

And then, somewhere in the wilderness surrounding the car park, she heard a dog barking. And Connor shouting, 'Simon? Where are you?'

'Simon?' thought Mustella, springing up. 'What's happened to Simon?' Her brother was the only human being she had any time for. She knew he was a true Sleeth at heart. It was just a pity he hadn't been born with her powers.

Mustella bounced down the caravan steps. She concentrated her mind. For a true Sleeth, after a bit of practice, it was as easy as blinking. By the bottom step she wasn't in human form. She had shrunk, so that all you could see of her was a shiver in the long grass.

The grass rippled as she flowed through it. Her sinuous body was covered in silky red hair. There was a creamy white patch of it on her chest. Her sharp teeth were deadly. She'd become small, about the length of your forearm. But, in the animal world, her ferocity was legendary. Her kind could kill much bigger prey than themselves. They could fight off, snarling, squealing and biting, much bigger attackers.

Mustella stopped. Her sleek, red head rose

above the grass. Her rubbery neck craned this way and that. Her sensitive whiskers quivered.

People have heard of werewolves. It's no wonder – werewolves are dumb and dis-organized. They don't keep secrets well. There are loads of books and films about them. The whole world knows about them. They're old news.

But, through the centuries, Sleeths have been much more cunning, more secretive – and smarter. They've guarded their secret so well that even now, in the twenty-first century, almost no one, outside the Sleeth family circle, knows about wereweasels.

Chapter Eleven

Connor looked round helplessly. He'd lost Simon and Snail Bot. The jungly wasteland had swallowed them up.

Scooter was sniffing the ground.

'Can you track them, Scooter?' whispered Connor urgently.

Simon wasn't particularly smelly. But Snail Bot's rotten-egg pong should be sniffable, even by a dog as daffy as Scooter.

'Go on, girl, sniff its scent,' said Connor as Scooter dashed off.

He should have known better. Scooter couldn't track a skunk in a rose garden. She barked joyously. She'd found something!

'That's an empty pizza box,' sighed Connor. 'Scooter, can't you do *anything* dogs are supposed to do?'

Robo Dog would have followed that trail,

relentlessly, with his sharp metal nose to the ground. He'd be an ace tracker. Connor's frustration and his fears for Grandad made him angry. 'I'd rather have Robo Dog than you,' he told Scooter. 'You're no help at all!'

Scooter leapt up, as if he were praising her, and tried to lick his face.

'Bad dog, get down!' said Connor, shoving her away. 'You need to learn some lessons from Robo Dog. He's a *proper* dog. And you're useless!'

Where was Robo Dog, anyway? Where did all these robots hang out when they weren't at Grandad's?

Connor wiped the dog spit off his hands on to some tall grass. Wait a second, there was already something smeared on the grass stem. Delicate, silvery threads that glinted in the sun.

'Simon,' breathed Connor. His snail-mad buddy left snail trails wherever he went, as his slimy companions crawled all over him, and clung to his clothes and hair.

'Come on, Scooter,' said Connor.

Like an eagle-eyed Native-American tracker, Connor found the same silvery smears on a branch, then on the top brick of a heap of rubble.

'He went this way!' he told Scooter.

Connor was so focused, looking so hard for slime clues, that he suddenly crashed into something. '*Ouch!*' He looked up, and up. It was the blank, grey wall of a building.

He backed off so he could see better.

It was the big building you could see from Grandad's bungalow. The one that wasn't derelict, like all the others, but looked as if it were still being used. Did Snail Bot go in there, to be repaired? And had Simon followed the smelly little machine?

But there were no windows and no doors. No way in that Connor could see. Like Grandad's bungalow, the place seemed to be sealed up tight. He put his ear to the wall. He heard a sort of low hum from inside. Something was happening in there!

'I'll walk round it,' thought Connor. 'See if I can find a way in.' He began walking in the shadow of its windowless grey walls.

Then, suddenly, Connor saw tremors in the long grass. Scooter whined piteously. 'Quiet, girl,' said Connor, putting his hand out to calm her. But he could feel the hairs prickling at the back of his neck.

What was happening? Now the whole weedy wasteland seemed to be alive. The grass was rippling in waves like a green sea. Connor saw a silver swarm crawling over a rotten log. What were they? Insects? They vanished into the grass again.

Connor heard a chirruping round his feet, like grasshoppers. He looked down.

'Toilet Bots!' he said.

Scooter yowled and shot off to hide.

Connor crouched down. What were the cute little bots doing out here, in the big wide world, so far from their toilet home?

Maybe they'd left the bungalow because Nurse Bot was such a tyrant.

Connor felt extra depressed. It was almost like rats leaving a sinking ship.

'Why didn't you stay with Grandad?' he asked them as they twittered round his feet, cleaning mud off his trainers with their loo-brush tails.

It must be really grim for Grandad in there now. Imprisoned with only Nurse Bot for company, and not even the cheery cleaning song of the Toilet Bots to greet him every time she made him go to the bathroom. But Connor could hardly blame the little bots for moving out. And, anyway, what could Toilet Bots do against Nurse Bot? She had such formidable powers.

He crouched down, let the little Toilet Bots trickle over his hand. Their tiny sucker feet tickled. 'Where are you going?' he asked them.

They weren't looking at him. Their pin-sized, glowing blue eyes were all fixed on the factory wall. They seemed to be on a mission.

'How'd you get out of Grandad's house?' asked Connor.

But he knew that it could have been through that tiny robot trapdoor, like Snail Bot. Or even through the ventilation grille. That wasn't a way in for him – or a way out for Grandad.

His mind suddenly flashed to what Simon had said. 'Mustella could get in through there.'

But Connor dismissed it. 'He was just talking rubbish.'

The Toilet Bots swarmed up to the blank, grey wall. There seemed like hundreds, even thousands of them! A vast herd of Toilet Bots

on the move, like migrating wildebeest –
only smaller. What were they going to do
now? It looked to Connor like a dead end.
But they stood waiting, twittering among
themselves.

Then suddenly, as if they'd ordered it, a
little door slid open in the wall.

The Toilet Bots poured through in a silver
stream. Connor didn't even think of following. This door was bigger than the one in
Grandad's bungalow. But it was obviously for
bots. Connor was tall, big for his age. There
was no way he could squeeze through.

Anyway, the bot door was already closing.
But just before it did, with a frantic howl,
Scooter rushed up to it.

'No, Scooter!' yelled Connor.

As usual, Scooter took no notice. As usual,
she was doing the wrong thing. She was
supposed to be running away from the nippy
little bots, not going in the same direction. But
the poor mixed-up pooch wriggled through
after them, on her belly.

The last Connor saw of her was a red
swishy tail, which she snatched out of the way
just in time as the bot door slid shut.

Connor rushed up to the bot door and

slid down on his knees. You could hardly
see where it had opened. Except, round the
edges, was a silvery smear of slime.

'Simon!' breathed Connor.

His buddy had gone this way, probably
following the damaged Snail Bot. Simon was
small and skinny enough to squeeze through
that door.

Connor scrambled to his feet, kicking at
the door in helpless rage. 'What's going on?'
he roared.

But who was there to answer him? Grandad was sealed up inside his bungalow,
Nurse Bot's prisoner. His buddy Simon had
disappeared into a sinister, windowless building after Snail Bot. Even Scooter had deserted
him. And he was left out here, on his own, in a
wilderness of weeds and crumbling car parks.

He listened. There was silence all around.
Except for the low hum of bees in some yellow
daisies. Connor had never felt more alone,
more bewildered and helpless.

Then the skin on his scalp crawled. He was
being watched, he was sure of it. And from
above . . .

His eyes gazed up into a treetop and
searched around. There!

From an old magpie's nest, two bright round eyes peered down at him. But it wasn't a bird. Connor saw a red streak flash down the tree trunk. He looked down baffled as the grass shook at his feet. Now, those same two glittering eyes peered *up* at him.

He couldn't help but stare back. Right into their depths. The world about him seemed to dissolve. Only the eyes existed for him, two searing pinpoints of light. He was totally in their power.

A terrible panic gripped him. He felt his heart beat faster, his whole body shaking. He was crouching in some kind of cramped, dark tunnel. He knew he should run, but he couldn't move; he was paralysed. A musty smell filled his nostrils. Something frightful was coming down the tunnel towards him. There was no escape!

'Hi,' came Mustella Sleeth's cool, sardonic voice.

Connor shook his head violently, trying to clear his fuddled brain. His fit of fear was already washing away. It had left him weak and trembling. But he was back in control of his own thoughts.

Mustella was standing there, right in front

of him, slipping on a pair of plastic flip-flops. He stared at her. 'Where'd you come from?'

'I was up that tree,' said Mustella.

Connor was too shaken to see it, but she was enjoying his confusion. She hadn't met a human yet she couldn't hypnotize while she changed from weasel to human form, or back again. No human ever saw a Sleeth transform; their weasel eyes made sure of that. Eyes that could mesmerize a rabbit, fix it to the spot, even as they were about to take its life.

And Mustella was even more talented than that. She could send mind pictures. She was proud of her powers. Humans were pathetic by comparison. She'd never met a human, outside her family, whom she had any respect for.

A wild recklessness came over her. She'd been in this dangerous, restless mood all day. 'I was in the magpie's nest,' she said, even though Connor didn't ask.

Weasels have secret hidcouts all over the place, where they rest when they're out hunting. And, often, the dens are lined with the fur or feathers of their victims to make them cosy. Mustella didn't only hunt rabbits. She snacked on birds, lizards, even insects, when no rabbits were around. She'd had a snug little den once, among tree roots, lined with the shiny blue wings of flying beetles.

It was even more vital for wereweasels to have dens. They prefer to change to weasel and back in the privacy of their houses or caravans, so clothes aren't a problem. But they all have secret clothes stashes, for emergencies, like Mustella had in the old magpie's nest. Naked Sleeths, wandering about the countryside, would have given their secret away long ago.

Connor had finally shaken off that feeling of doom, with the idea that he was going to die and there was nothing he could do about it. His mind was sharper now. And he was thinking, 'This girl's just having a laugh, making a fool out of me.'

There *was* an easy grin on Mustella's face. It wasn't spiteful. It just seemed to say, 'Don't even *try* to understand – you haven't got a hope.'

So why did she feel an awful temptation creeping over her to tell Connor the truth? She fought it back. Did her usual trick of flashing mind pictures into his brain, to make him terrified again, just like a hunted rabbit.

But this time Connor was prepared. When those feelings of shivering doom tried to overpower him, he resisted. He'd had plenty of practice lately, ever since Grandad got rushed to hospital, fighting off panicky feelings that Grandad was going to die at any moment . . .

He did that now. With a superhuman effort, he pushed away those dark and frightening mind pictures. Mustella felt a barrier go up in his mind.

She was amazed. That had never happened before. She gave a shrill, weasel cry of anger. Weasels aren't used to being defeated. They're ferocious fighters; they take on attackers much bigger than themselves, even badgers and wolves. They fight to the death and never, ever surrender.

Mustella was hopping mad. 'I'll show him,' she thought. 'Who does he think he is, standing up to *me*?' And in one crazy, thoughtless moment she threw caution to the winds.

'Look into my eyes,' she ordered Connor.

'No,' said Connor, deliberately looking away. She'd tried that once too often. Did she think he was stupid? He didn't know how Mustella did it – how she made him feel afraid like that. But it was obvious that it

131

all started when you stared into her eyes.

Mustella felt herself getting agitated. She wasn't used to having her victims argue with her either. 'OK,' she said grudgingly. 'I won't do that again, that mind-picture thing.' There wasn't much point anyway, when Connor could resist it.

Connor wasn't convinced. He didn't mean to look into her eyes. But somehow he couldn't help it. They drew his gaze like a magnet.

But Mustella stuck to her promise and, this time, when he looked at her, Connor didn't feel fear. He was aware of the world going blurry, like before. His head was spinning. But then it all stopped. He unlocked his eyes from hers and found that Mustella had vanished and in her place was a weasel, poking its head out of a small heap of clothes: shorts, a T-shirt with a blue sequin heart and two pink plastic flip-flops.

Connor shook his head in shock. It wasn't possible. But the weasel didn't run away. It stood on its hind legs, its body long and sinuous as a snake's. It stared at him. It had Mustella's bright alert eyes, her red silky hair and her small, neat, round head.

'Don't be ridiculous,' Connor told himself.

But then those weasel eyes held his gaze again. He couldn't look away. And when he was released he saw Mustella. She was slipping on her flip-flops. And the weasel? It wasn't there any more.

But Mustella hadn't noticed she'd put her T-shirt on the wrong way round, with the blue sequin heart at the back.

Connor's head was reeling. He felt he'd totally lost touch with reality.

'I'm a wereweasel,' said Mustella, with pride in her voice.

But, even as she said it, she was thinking, 'You've done it now. Dad'll go ballistic!'

Weasels aren't scared of anything. But the awful consequences of what she'd just said were making even Mustella tremble. She must have been mad. She'd told a stranger the Sleeth family secret. She hadn't just told him, she'd given him a demonstration. Out of vanity, just to score some points. To get back at him because he could resist her mind pictures.

And she'd really opened the floodgates. Connor just couldn't shut up. 'Change back!' he said. 'Do it again!'

'It's not a *trick*,' said Mustella, suddenly uncooperative and sullen.

'But it's amazing, incredible,' raved Connor. He was absolutely gobsmacked. 'Is it magic?'

Mustella rolled her eyes. 'Don't be silly.'

'What is it, then?'

'Some people say it's a genetic mutation. We *true* Sleeths say it's a gift.'

'I can't believe it,' said Connor, shaking his head helplessly. He'd known there was something weird about Mustella from the first moment he saw her. But not this weird.

He had a million questions buzzing around like flies in his brain. 'Can Simon do it?'

'No,' said Mustella. 'Not all Sleeths inherit it. I was just lucky.'

She wished he'd stop asking about it. All the time, the horror of what she'd just done was growing. As soon as they could talk, every Sleeth was warned, 'Tell no one!' It was as good as burned into their brains, engraved on their hearts. '*Tell no one. Not ever.*' And she'd just gone and told. She'd betrayed every wereweasel in Great Britain. 1,012 of them when they were last counted at the annual wereweasel gathering.

'What about clothes?' Connor was saying. 'Do you carry them with you?'

'Don't be silly,' said Mustella, even more scornfully.

'What do you eat?' asked Connor.

Mustella shrugged. 'Pizzas, pasta and stuff. Just like you.' She didn't tell him about the rabbits she ate raw, when she was in weasel form. Or the worms and frogs she snacked on.

She didn't mention either that she could kill small prey like mice and voles and baby rabbits with a single bite to the back of the neck. But often she didn't need to because when they saw her, or even when they just smelt her, they died of fright.

But she was tired of stupid questions. And scared too, because Connor just wouldn't shut up.

'You mustn't talk about it,' she said suddenly.

'But –?'

'No!' said Mustella frantically. 'You mustn't talk about it. Mustn't ask me things. I shouldn't have told you!'

'But –?' said Connor.

'This isn't some magic trick,' insisted

Mustella. 'It's serious. It's what we are. It's our lives! If other people find out . . .'

She could hardly speak. Once the world knew, wereweasels like her would be hounded, never let alone. The press would be banging on their doors, and doctors would try to 'cure' them. They'd say, 'With modern scientific methods we can weed out mutant embryos. No more wereweasel babies need be born!' True Sleeths would soon become extinct. Connor just didn't understand.

But, to her surprise, Connor looked at her with sympathy. 'They'd call you freaks, wouldn't they?' he said.

He thought she might explode, 'How dare you?' But she just nodded gratefully and said, 'It'd be worse than that. Wereweasels' embryos would be selected out – like we don't deserve to live! Just because we're different.'

'I won't tell,' promised Connor. 'You needn't be afraid.'

'I'm not,' said Mustella indignantly. No one ever accused wereweasels of being afraid. But, in her human form she *was* afraid; she just couldn't help it.

'I-I shouldn't have told you,' she said. 'Just

don't talk about it any more. Right? Not to me. Not to anyone.'

Connor struggled to cool down his boiling brain. More questions were bubbling up all the time. The whole wereweasel thing was so mind-boggling, so unbelievable. Yet it had happened, right in front of his eyes!

But he could see from her scowling face that more questions were forbidden.

With a massive effort, he wrenched his mind away from weasels back to all his other worries. And, when he did, he thought, 'How could I have forgotten Grandad for so long?'

And what about Simon?

'Your brother's just gone in there,' he said, jerking his thumb towards the factory building.

'What?' said Mustella, who'd temporarily forgotten about Simon too. 'What's he gone in there for?'

'He's gone after Snail Bot,' said Connor. 'He wants to destroy it. And find out who made it.'

'Eh?' said Mustella, wrinkling her weasly button nose as if she was sniffing a rabbit.

'Hasn't Simon told you about my grandad and Nurse Bot and Snail Bot?'

'Nurse Bot? What *are* you on about?' Mustella's neck craned this way and that. It suddenly struck her that, when she and Simon met, the talk was all about her weasel life. She never felt any interest in his human life or in his personal thoughts or problems. After all, she was the special one.

Connor took a deep breath.

'Well,' he began, 'it all started when Mrs Dixon made me and Simon buddies . . .' And then he gave Mustella a quick rundown of the trouble Grandad was in and how Simon had somehow got himself mixed up in it.

'And Simon just went berserk when he saw Snail Bot,' finished Connor. 'And he followed it in there.'

He didn't tell Mustella that Scooter was in there too, and the Toilet Bots. Explaining Nurse Bot had been hard enough. He just couldn't *begin* to describe the Toilet Bots. In the present crisis there just wasn't the time. Besides, Mustella didn't care about them or Scooter. Simon was all she cared about.

Connor felt the full force of her hypnotic gaze. It seemed to hold his eyes in a vice; the world around went blurry, then, suddenly, it released him.

And he saw a weasel, leaping through the long grass, its body arching like a tiny red rainbow.

It was Mustella, running round the building, looking for a way in. Weasels always find a way in. Their prey doesn't stand a chance. They can squeeze themselves through the tiniest crannies.

'When you get inside,' yelled Connor, 'open the door for me!'

Did she hear? In her weasel form, could she understand? Connor had no idea. It was crazy enough anyway, talking to a weasel. But he knew it was Mustella. There were her clothes, in a heap in the grass.

'Let me in!' yelled Connor as Mustella bounded out of sight round the corner of the building. Even if she heard and understood, she might not do what he wanted. Weasels are a law unto themselves.

Connor stood there, totally confused, his mind in turmoil. He felt more out of control than ever. If she'd waited to discuss it with him, he'd have asked Mustella to get into Grandad's first, through that ventilation grille.

But what should he do now? Should he wait here? Even if Mustella found a way into the building, would she let him in? Who could read Mustella's mind or predict what she would do?

Should he go back to Grandad's bungalow? But what could he do there? Nurse Bot had the place so well defended, he'd probably need a tank to break in.

Connor stood there, undecided, jigging from one foot to the other. He was even chewing his nails and he hadn't done that for years.

'I wish Grandad had never picked up that brochure,' he was thinking. 'I wish he'd never heard of Friendly Domestic Robots.'

Chapter Twelve

'Oh no,' Simon moaned to himself.

He'd lost sight of Snail Bot. When he'd wriggled after it, before the bot door slid shut, he was right behind it. So close that the blasts from its back end almost made him pass out. Snail Bot's eggy pong still lingered in the air. But somehow Snail Bot had escaped him.

He looked around. 'Which way did it go?'

Inside, the building was like a maze. There were dusty corridors going off in all directions. And they all looked exactly the same. Opening off from each of them were the same rows of tiny cell-like rooms that must once have been offices. But they were empty now, with all their shelves ripped out and computer desks taken away.

And it was gloomy too. Tiny, feeble yellow lights flickered from the corridor ceiling. But in between them were deep pools of blackness where you'd have to feel your way along the walls.

He peered into an office cubicle. This one wasn't quite empty. There was a single sad, forgotten chair in a corner. And a torn calendar from years ago, flapping on a noticeboard.

'That Snail Bot could be anywhere,' thought Simon.

It would take him ages to search for it, in all these corridors, all these dusty cells. Simon shivered. This place was eerie; a ghost building. It had once been busy, full of people working. Now it was an empty, echoing shell.

He suddenly felt very lost. He wasn't sure he could find his way back to the bot door. And even if he could, could he get out? Like the doors in Connor's grandad's bungalow it had no handles, or buttons to push. It seemed that only bots could open it.

He was scared too, trapped in this spooky, echoing building. Why had he run ahead of his buddy and plunged through the bot door on his own? 'Wish I'd waited for Connor,' he thought.

Simon had no idea that he wasn't alone in

the building. That, somewhere in this rabbit warren of rooms and corridors, as well as Snail Bot, were Dr Darlick, Scooter and the Toilet Bots. Even Robo Dog was in here somewhere, waiting to get his creaky knee joints oiled.

Simon had no idea either that his sister, Mustella, in weasel form, had just found a way in. At that very moment, she was squeezing between the sharp blades of an extractor fan. While Connor was biting his nails outside, desperate for her to let him in so that he could find his buddy, and Scooter. And, with any luck, the lunatic who'd invented Nurse Bot. What sort of twisted mind could have created her? Connor couldn't even *begin* to imagine.

'It's my birthday today,' thought Simon, feeling terribly sorry for himself. What a way to celebrate it, trapped in this creepy place.

Then he felt a tiny tickling. He looked down. It was his tiniest, most fragile snail, with the shell like yellow, frosted glass. It was crawling across the back of his hand, as if it was trying to tell him something. Its silvery trail sparkled on his skin.

'*Awww!*' said Simon. It was so small and frail; its shell so brittle. Snail Bot would have minced it up in a second. Yet it was so adventurous! This tiny snail made epic journeys that in human terms would have been like trekking to the North or South Poles. It crawled up into his hair. Sometimes he found it nestling inside his socks when he took them off.

Simon's face grew grim with determination.

'I won't let you down,' he told the plucky little explorer. He put it back gently to join the other snails in a sticky clot in his pocket.

'SOS. Save Our Snails,' Simon ordered himself.

He stopped shivering. His spine stiffened. He felt strength flood back into his body. He shrugged off his fears, his feelings of self-pity. His mission was to destroy Snail Bot and make sure its inventor didn't make any more of the evil, snail-crushing machines.

'And that,' murmured Simon, reminding himself of what he'd thought last night, 'would be my best birthday present, ever.'

But which direction should he go in? Everywhere looked the same – bare rooms like empty boxes; dismal, dimly lit corridors stretching away into darkness.

Simon turned a corner – more corridors!

Then, suddenly, he heard it: a low humming. The same humming that Connor had heard from outside, when he put his ear to the building.

Simon screwed up his face in concentration: 'Where's it coming from?' It sounded like distant machinery, or computers. He swivelled round. Then swivelled again.

He finally decided, 'I think it's coming from *that* direction.'

Then, in the gloomy distance he saw, or thought he saw, a haze of stars rushing by, in a silver stream. For a few seconds, they covered the floor, the walls and the ceiling – the whole corridor seemed to sparkle with silver spangles. And with them came a strange, high, twittering sound, like a caveful of bats. Simon blinked, and looked again. They were gone.

And the only sound he could hear now was humming.

Wait a bit. From somewhere quite near, came another sound. It was a long melancholy howl. The most lonesome, heartbroken yowling he'd ever heard.

'*Yowww – owww-owww!*'

'Scooter?' wondered Simon.

But how could it be her? She was safe outside, with Connor.

He listened. The howl didn't come again. He didn't see any rushing stars either. 'This place gives me the creeps,' thought Simon. 'It's playing tricks with my mind.'

But, 'Stay cool,' he warned himself. He must keep his mind on his mission. The snails of the world were depending on him. He must try to track down that humming. It was his only clue.

He set off, down the long, gloomy corridor.

Unlike Simon, the Toilet Bots knew exactly where they were going. And they couldn't afford to waste time. They had some energy supplies stored up. But they would have to find more fuel soon.

They rushed, like an eager insect swarm, through the maze of empty corridors. With their strong sucker feet they could cling to the walls or the ceiling. Their tiny blue eyes glowed like sapphires in the dark.

They were heading for a room where there was a computer. It had been left behind because it was broken. But the Toilet Bots had fixed it. They were computer wizards as well as toilet cleaners. They were ace engineers too. On their way to the room, they'd collected some more titanium, nickel and other materials they needed to replicate themselves. They'd snatched them from Dr Darlick's research lab, right under his nose. He'd been too busy talking to the photo of Nanny McFiggins to notice.

The Toilet Bot tribe was growing. And they had plans. They weren't content any more to clean Grandad's toilet, which is what Dr Darlick had invented them for. Their tiny robot brains had far greater ambitions.

Some of them had visited this building several times, to surf the Net or nick materials from Dr Darlick's research lab. But he'd never seen them. When he wasn't consulting Nanny, he was glued to a computer screen, watching Nurse Bot turn Grandad's brain to soup. Besides, it never occurred to him that some of his robots might be out of control. That they might have minds of their own. You especially wouldn't expect it of humble little loo cleaners.

The Toilet Bots clustered round the computer.

Some scuttled over the keys, looking for

websites. Pictures came up on the screen. One was a map of the sewage system of central London. Each little bot stored that information in its robot brain. Then came another picture.

The little bots' eyes glowed brighter with wonder.

'Cheep, cheep, cheep, cheep.'

They chirruped among themselves, in Toilet Bot language, excitedly.

Then, like a rippling silver sea, they rushed off again, down empty corridors, towards the bot door.

'Yowwww – owww-owww!'

That was Scooter. She'd just met the bot tribe again, for the second time in ten minutes. They surged past her. Dogs didn't interest them. They were too busy following their dreams.

But Scooter wasn't taking any chances. Her nose was still stinging from her first encounter with the grippy little cleaners, in Grandad's toilet bowl. She hurtled off, howling, and hid in an empty office.

Outside, the Toilet Bots scuttled through the long grass. Until, near a derelict building, they found a manhole cover. Muscular tree roots had heaved it half up. Like a glittering silver waterfall, the little robots poured down, into the sewers.

Back in the office they'd just been in, the computer was still humming to itself. The Toilet Bots had left in too much of a hurry to close it down. The last picture they'd looked at, their eyes bright with wonder, was still on the computer screen.

It was a picture of Buckingham Palace.

Chapter Thirteen

C onnor watched the Toilet Bots come out of the bot door and stream away through the long grass.

'Where are they off to now?' he wondered.

They seemed to know. But it was dangerous out there for little cleaning bots. What did they know about the big, wide world? They'd lived all their lives in a toilet bowl!

Connor would have been worried about them. But there just wasn't room in his mind, not with all his other worries.

'*Pssst!*' said a voice. 'Come in here. You won't believe what I've found!'

'Mustella!'

A door had opened in the blank, grey wall of the building. Not a door for small bots this time, but human size. And Mustella, in human form, was poking her head round it. '*Pssst!* Hurry up!'

Connor went racing over and slid inside. Mustella had found a white laboratory coat from somewhere and bundled herself up in it. It reached to her ankles and the sleeves were long and dangly. The too-big coat made her look vulnerable somehow and less scary. But her weasel eyes still glittered at him with fierce brightness. She dashed in front of him: 'This way!'

The humming sound, which Connor had heard faintly through the walls, was much louder now that he was inside the building. And, as he followed Mustella up a long flight of steps, the hum became the grinding roar of machinery.

. They went through another door. They were on a sort of metal platform, high above the floor, looking down on a vast room.

Connor had a bird's-eye view of a factory workshop spread out below them. The activity and the racket were overwhelming; the neon lights were as harsh and as bright as in an operating theatre. The workshop stretched away into the shadowy distance, where the lights didn't reach. It was such a huge space you couldn't see where it ended. At first, Connor couldn't make sense of what he was seeing.

There were long, rumbling conveyor belts. Huge robot arms swung over them like cranes, lifting, drilling and welding with their great claw hands. He couldn't see any human workers down there, only machines. Some robot arms, with long, sensitive fingers, were assembling electrical circuits. What were they making?

Connor saw thin, shiny plates of metal. He saw a whole line of skull faces like silver masks. He saw eyeballs, joggling along a conveyor belt. And red tubes, wriggling like worms, being sliced up into lip lengths.

'*Oh no*,' he breathed.

'They're making Nurse Bots,' he told Mustella in an appalled voice.

But he'd almost forgotten, how could she appreciate the full horror of what was happening down there? Mustella had never even *seen* Nurse Bot, let alone experienced her awesome powers. How she could make your mind into mush and imprison you inside your home. And stop the people who loved you from getting in to rescue you.

'She could probably stop a whole *army* from getting in to rescue you,' thought Connor.

But then Connor realized someone else was beside him, staring down at the assembly line, just as horrified as he was.

'Simon!' said Connor and Mustella at the same time.

Simon had been tracking the hum through the endless corridors and had at last found the right door. He turned round as if he'd only just noticed them. 'What are you two doing here?'

'Looking for you,' said Mustella. 'And now we've found you let's get out of here.'

'No!' said Connor and Simon both together.

'What about my grandad?' said Connor. 'And what about Scooter? She's in here somewhere.'

'And what about Snail Bot?' Simon chipped in. He still hadn't found the foul-smelling, murdering little robot. And now he was even more worried. A production line that could make Nurse Bots could easily assemble Snail Bots. Soon, every gardener in the country would have one!

'We've got to find out who's running this

operation,' Connor was explaining to Mustella. 'And make them stop. Because they're evil.'

'*Evil*,' echoed Simon, nodding in grim agreement.

Mustella wrinkled her nose in disgust. She hated this alien world of noise and machinery and shiny metal. She hated this big, brightly lit space. Her weasel world was a secretive, dark world of dens and tunnels. It smelt of earth and blood and fur. And the only sound was the scream of her prey as she went for their throats.

She felt powerless here. You can't hypnotize machines, or send them scary mind pictures, or go for their jugular. But still she pointed out a door down on the factory floor. The notice on it said: 'Dr Charles Darlick, Research Lab. Strictly No Admittance.'

'Who?' said Connor. He couldn't remember a Dr Charles Darlick being mentioned in the Friendly Domestic Robots brochure. But could *he* be the human brain behind all this? Could that lab be the nerve centre for this whole operation?

'I want to see in there,' said Connor. 'Come on!'

There was a flight of iron steps leading to

another platform. Then a second flight led right down to the factory floor. Connor and Simon started clattering down, their boots ringing on the metal. Mustella hesitated. There was a bitter struggle going on inside her. Should she change into weasel form and wriggle out through the nearest extractor fan? Go back to her own world where she was a powerful, top predator? None of this was any of her business. It was human business – they could sort out their own mess. What did she care about that stupid dog, or Connor's grandad?

But the trouble was, Simon had somehow got himself mixed up in it. And she *did* care about him. And Connor couldn't be ignored, however much she'd like that, because she'd told him the Sleeth family secret.

'You must have been crazy,' Mustella raged at herself. 'Why did you do that?' She couldn't even remember now. But Connor was like a walking time bomb. If he told the secret, the consequences would be terrible. And he was doubly dangerous, because she couldn't scare him with mind pictures.

Mustella was a wild, free wereweasel. She was proud of the fact that no human, not even

Simon, had any hold over her. But now she'd bound herself to Connor with hoops of steel. He'd said he wouldn't tell – but she didn't trust him. She didn't trust any humans.

'You got to stay with him,' she told herself. 'Keep an eye on him. Make sure he keeps his mouth shut.' With every fibre of her being, she longed to transform, escape back to weasel world where she feared nothing, where she felt in control. But she had to stay human.

'You coming, sis?' Simon yelled back at her.

Simon did wonder, briefly, why she was wearing a white coat that was miles too big for her. Had she just changed back from being a wereweasel? Had Connor been any-where near? But Simon knew he didn't have to worry. Whatever had happened, the Sleeth family secret would be safe. Mustella would never reveal it, not in a million years. She was the strong one. He was the one who always had to watch himself, in case he blurted it out.

'I'm coming,' said Mustella. But her voice was no more than a whisper. It was drowned out by the roar of machinery.

Mustella followed them down. She couldn't dart, weasel-quick, like she usually did, even in human form. The lab coat was so long and draggy she was scared she'd trip over it. She was used to feeling grass and soft soil under her bare feet. But here the sharp metal edges of the steps cut into them.

She'd just joined Simon and Connor on the next platform, still high above the manic activity down below. Suddenly red lights began flashing all around them.

'What's going on?' said Simon.

At the same time, all the machines stopped. Great robot arms hung suspended in the air, their claws dangling. The rumbling conveyor belts were still.

Connor leaned over the platform rails, staring down. After the deafening racket the silence should have been welcome. But instead the hush was spooky, loaded with menace as if something wicked was on its way.

Then, from the gloom beyond the production line, somewhere at the back of the vast space where the bright lights didn't penetrate, came a humming sound. Connor's ears twitched.

But Simon didn't seem to notice. 'I'm going down,' he said impatiently. 'What are we standing here for?' He was all fired up to meet the evil inventor of Snail Bot. He wouldn't be timid and tongue-tied and wary then, like he usually was with people.

'I've got a few things I want to say to that guy,' said Simon. His pale little old man's face scrunched up into such a ferocious scowl that Mustella stared at him, amazed. She'd never seen him like this before. She realized that she hardly knew her little brother at all.

Simon started down the last flight of steps.

'No!' said Connor, holding him back. 'Something's happening!'

Connor had recognized that humming. It made his skin crawl. But he'd never heard it this loud before. It was swelling, growing louder. It rose into the air like a swarm of killer bees.

The flashing red lights stopped. The bright white lights over the conveyor belts dimmed. Connor swallowed nervously. It seemed like the show was about to start.

Suddenly, those distant shadows were seething with life. A silver flash, a goggly eyeball, the eerie blue glow of computer screens, a scraggy hank of hair . . .

'Nurse Bots,' said Connor, licking dry lips.

Then, as if at a single command, they came

surging out of the darkness, row after row of them, in perfect formation.

'What are those freaky machines?' thought Mustella, craning her snaky neck. She hissed defiance, and gave a high weasel scream of anger. But, this time, it didn't work. For the first time in her life, she felt like running away from something.

'Are they coming to get us?' asked Simon, close to panic. Even the little yellow snail nestled in his hair was waving its antennae anxiously.

Still more Nurse Bots came, gliding round the conveyor belts, until the front rank stopped, right under the platform they were standing on. Now they filled the whole factory, packed every spare bit of floor space, like a grotesque army on parade.

'There's loads of them!' said Connor, his voice cracking with horror. 'There's hundreds of them!'

He stared down at a sea of scraggy wigs, with patches of silver skull showing through, stretching right back to the distant, shadowy recesses at the far end of the workshop.

The Nurse Bot army's goggly eyes glared. Their bushy brows glowered. 'NURSE BOT

CAN SEE YOU' flashed up, at exactly the same second, on all their computer screens.

'They are!' gibbered Simon. 'They're after us!'

Up on the metal platform, the three huddled together.

'It's a nightmare,' thought Connor, gazing down on the massed Nurse Bots. One was bad enough. But now she'd been multiplied, hundreds of times.

'Let's get out of here!' said Simon. They clattered back up to the top platform, yanked the door handle. The door had locked itself behind them. 'We're trapped,' said Simon.

'Can those things climb stairs?' asked Mustella, looking back down.

'No,' said Simon. 'As long as we stay up here, we're safe.'

'No, we're not,' said Connor. 'This platform is metal. The stairs are metal.'

Simon stared at him, bewildered for a second. Then he understood. 'Your grandad's Nurse Bot,' he gasped. 'She had electric fingers!' One touch from them and he'd have gone up in smoke. If these Nurse Bots were like Connor's grandad's, and they looked identical, all it would take was one touch, from one Nurse Bot's silver talon, to turn the steps and platform they were standing on into a high-voltage death trap.

Simon lost his head. 'Save yourself,' he gabbled at Mustella. 'Transform! Get out of here! There must be a gap you can squeeze through.'

Then he stopped, appalled. What was he saying? He clamped a hand over his mouth. Had he let slip the Sleeth family secret? Simon's eyes sent a silent, beseeching question to his sister, 'I didn't let it slip, did I?'

Behind Connor's back, Mustella mouthed her reply.

'What?' Simon mouthed back, in shocked disbelief. Because, as Mustella's lips moved, he thought he made out the words, 'He already knows.'

That was far too explosive to deal with, especially right now. So Simon decided, 'Nah, I'm just rubbish at lip reading. She can't have meant that.' He concentrated instead on what Connor was saying.

'I don't think they're after us,' said Connor, still staring down at the Nurse Bots.

'How do you know?' asked Simon.

'Look for yourself,' said Connor.

Simon leaned over the platform rail and gazed down on the rows of robots.

'I don't think they know we're here,' said Connor. 'They're not even looking at us.'

Suddenly, a tinny, mechanical voice shrilled out from somewhere, 'Testing! Testing!'

Instantly, the vast army responded like one Nurse Bot. Thousands of red rubbery lips writhed and squirmed into self-satisfied smirks. Silver talons crossed smugly on skirt fronts. On a thousand computer screens the words flashed up:

NURSE BOT KNOWS BEST

Then their yakky voices swelled in chorus, echoing the words on their screens: '*Nurse Bot knows best. Nurse Bot knows best. Nurse Bot knows best.*' The sinister chant, from a thousand metal throats, in a Scottish accent, sent shivers down Connor's spine.

Then the robots fell silent. Their faces immobile, they stared straight ahead.

'Hey, Nurse Bots!' Connor yelled down. 'Up here!' He waved. 'Up here!'

Not a single wobbly eyeball swivelled upwards.

'See?' said Connor. 'They're not interested in us.'

They hadn't been sent out specially to find and destroy. Connor guessed they weren't fully operational. They were still being put through routine tests, as part of their programming.

'*Phew*,' said Simon. 'Shall we go down there? Think we can risk it?'

'We've got to,' said Connor. Going down to the factory floor was their only way out. And, anyway, he badly wanted a peek in that research lab. Would Dr Charles Darlick be in there?

Like Simon, Connor wanted a few words with that guy. He wanted him to stop this whole experiment and set Grandad free from his robot 'carer'. Could Dr Darlick do it? 'He'd better be able to,' thought Connor grimly. Surely *someone* could control that metal tyrant?

And what about all these other Nurse Bots? What did Dr Darlick need them for? But Connor didn't have time to think about that now. Grandad was his main concern. And Scooter was second on his list. Where *was* that pea-brained pooch?

'Come on,' said Connor, clanging down the

iron stairs with Simon close behind. Simon's outrage at the evil Snail Bot drove him on. But he couldn't help flinching when he got down to floor level and began to thread his way through the Nurse Bot army. That terrible transformation, outside Grandad's bungalow, when Nurse Bot went into attack mode, was still fresh in his mind.

The most reluctant was Mustella, squirming inside her human skin, longing to be her weasel self. She hated feeling so scared, so out of her depth, so like any *ordinary* human child. None of her special powers was any use here. Here, the machines ruled.

But she had to stick with the two boys. Especially that buddy of Simon's – she had to watch his every move.

'What are you going to do?' she fumed at herself. 'Follow him round all his *life* to make sure he doesn't tell?' Pity he wasn't a rabbit. Then she could have killed him easily. One bite to the back of his neck and – problem solved.

Raging inside at her own helplessness, she padded after Simon and Connor on her tender bare feet, down to the factory floor.

Chapter Fourteen

Simon crept among the Nurse Bots. He was trying to find the research lab of Dr Charles Darlick. It had been easy to spot from the high platform. But now, in these rows of identical robots, he'd lost his sense of direction. He'd lost sight of Mustella and Connor as well.

The Nurse Bots seemed deactivated. They were silent, not even humming. Their chest computer screens were dark. They stood stiffly to attention, eyes front, arms down by their sides. Simon glanced nervously up at the nearest Nurse Bot face. The red wormy lips didn't squirm, or the bushy eyebrows twitch, or the eyeballs swivel. It was as still and lifeless as a death mask.

The whole factory was spookily silent as Simon tiptoed through the bots. It seemed suspended in time. The great robot arms were still at rest, dangling over the stopped conveyor belts. The only sound he could hear was his own heart hammering. He jumped. What was that squeal? But it was only his rubber trainer soles on the floor.

He tried desperately to ignore the Nurse Bots all around him. They were taller than him, adult-size, so unless he looked up, he didn't have to see their faces. But his eyes couldn't avoid those silver talons hanging by their stiff metal skirts. Everywhere he looked he saw Nurse Bot fingers, jointed like crab legs, more fingers . . .

Were the bots moving? Were they crowding in on him? Simon looked up, his heart beating so hard it seemed to be crashing against his ribs.

'Get a grip!' he told himself sternly. 'They're shut down.' Their metal faces were empty, totally without expression. They were just machines. It was hard to believe Grandad's Nurse Bot had seemed so horribly alive and human and full of malice.

Just thinking of Grandad's Nurse Bot made Simon sneak a hand into his pocket and get out his biggest snail, the one he used as a worry bead. Stroking the banded orange and brown shell calmed him down. And made him remember why he was here in the first place.

'SOS. Save Our Snails,' he muttered to himself. He had to destroy Snail Bot. And stop any more from being made. That was his top priority. He was angry with himself that, for a moment there, he'd taken his eye off the ball.

'You're looking for this Darlick guy,' Simon reminded himself. He could be the brain behind all these bots. But where on earth was his lab? Simon couldn't tell, lost in a forest of Nurse Bots that, like pine trees, all looked the same. And where had his buddy and his big sister got to?

Gently, Simon put his worry-bead snail back into his pocket to join its sticky companions.

'Connor? Mustella?' he called from the factory floor, where he was hidden among the Nurse Bots. 'Where are you? I think I'm lost.' He called softly. But his voice sounded eerily loud in the church-like hush.

Then another voice shattered the silence. 'Testing! Testing!' Its parrot-like squawk ripped through the air. Simon's heart hammered all over again. He stared around but it was OK, false alarm, nothing was happening. He could breathe easily.

He was between two rows of bots, about to creep onwards. But then, right along the row, at the same second, the chest computer screens snapped on, with a sinister blue glow.

Hummm. That killer bee hum filled the air.

And the same words, in big flashing capitals, leapt on to every screen:

INTRUDER! ALARM! ALARM!

Then the world went manic. Hundreds of bot mouths gaped into wide red caves. That wailing air-raid siren sound almost burst Simon's eardrums. Cringing, he dropped to a crouch, clamped his hands over his ears and stared fearfully upwards. Eyeballs blazed above him, rubber lips writhed into snarls. *Sssss!*

The Nurse Bots seemed to rise up on their toes. How did they do that? They had no toes! They towered over him and at exactly the same moment they raised their arms high, hooked their hands into lethal weapons. Sparks flew out, as if their fingers were fireworks. They lurched forward, like tigers about to pounce . . .

On hands and knees Simon scuttled between their shiny metal skirts, trying to escape, or at least find a safe corner. The bots wailed and snarled. Showers of blue sparks drifted down. The bots were spinning and clashing like dodgem cars. Two almost crushed him! He saw a gap, dived towards it and crouched trembling against a wall while the mayhem raged above him. But he wasn't safe here. A bot rocked forward, its eyeballs jiggling grotesquely, its face a hate-filled grimace. Claw hands lunged at him, stabbing downwards, shooting out sizzling sparks.

'No!' screamed Simon, rolling up like a hedgehog, covering his head with his hands.

But, instead of being fried, he found himself suddenly hauled backwards. In a blind panic now, he struggled, kicking out.

'*Ow!*' said a voice. 'That hurt!'

Simon stopped fighting and went limp. Why was it so dark? He realized his eyes were still screwed tight shut. He forced them open.

'Hello,' said Mustella.

'The Nurse Bots! The Nurse Bots!'

gibbered Simon, getting ready to dive under a table. 'I can hear them humming!'

'It's OK,' said Connor. 'That's only computers.'

At last, Simon dared to look around. Connor was right. They were in a room crammed with bleeping, whirring computers. But no Nurse Bots.

'They're all outside,' explained Connor. In fact, it had gone very quiet out there. Connor opened the door a chink, risked a look.

'No, no,' moaned Simon. 'Don't let them in. They're after me.'

'They weren't after you,' said Connor. 'They weren't after anyone. They were just being tested. And you got mixed up in it.'

These Nurse Bots needed a lot more work before they had the brain power of Grandad's bot. But what would happen when they did? When they'd been fully programmed with all her spirit-crushing talents, her terror tactics and her spiteful tricks? Connor shuddered. Just what did Friendly Domestic Robots plan to do with all these metal monsters it was making?

Whatever it was, they were already making more of them. The assembly line was up and running again, the conveyor belts rumbling and the great robot arms swinging.

The testing was obviously over for now. And, as Connor watched, the Nurse Bot army was gliding silently back into the shadows, to wherever they were stored, their skull faces empty again and their computer screens dark and closed down.

But nothing could convince Simon that those mad robots weren't programmed to destroy him, personally.

'Close the door,' he begged Connor.

For the first time, Simon took notice of his surroundings. He'd been snatched to safety from the Nurse Bots, but where had he ended up? He was surrounded by banks of bleeping computers, and steel benches covered with wires and microchips that looked like bits of robot brains.

'Where are we?' he asked.

Mustella didn't answer. She'd picked up a book with a hideous red and green cover. She was reading it, very slowly, because she wasn't too hot at reading. It's not a skill weasels need, much. But something in the book shocked her. Because, with each page, her button nose twitched in disgust.

'We're in Doctor Darlick's research lab,' Connor told Simon.

'So where is he?' asked Simon.

Connor frowned. 'Don't know,' he started to say. But then Simon caught sight of a photo on the wall. He pointed at it with a trembling hand. 'N-Nur-Nurse Bot!' he quavered.

Connor went to look. It looked strange, out of place, having this old, faded photo among all the gleaming hi-tech equipment. And from a distance, you might have thought it was a Nurse Bot. It had the same scraggy, scraped-back hair, the same bushy brows, goggly eyes and tapeworm lips.

But when Connor peered at it more closely he told Simon, 'It's a person.' The woman in the picture had real human skin, not a face made out of steel. You could see her wrinkly neck. And, anyway, it obviously wasn't a Nurse Bot, because underneath the photo it said, 'Nanny McFiggins can see you.'

'It's someone called Nanny McFiggins,' said Connor.

'Well, she looks like a Nurse Bot,' said Simon, shuddering. 'She looks just as creepy.'

And then, after a long silence, Mustella spoke up. 'She's creepy all right,' she said.

'You ought to read this book. It says on the front *The Wisdom of Nanny McFiggins*. But it's the biggest load of old twaddle I've ever read!'

She snapped the book shut and sent it skimming over the desk top. It fell off the edge on to the floor.

'How dare you!' shrieked a scandalized voice. A hunched figure scurried from a side room. It dived for the book, scooped it off the floor, dusted it off, then nursed it as if to make it better.

'How dare you treat dear Nanny's book with such disrespect?' the figure screeched in outraged tones. 'How dare you say that her wisdom is a load of old twaddle?'

Chapter Fifteen

Connor stared at the gnome-like figure, cuddling its book like a comfort blanket and stamping its tiny feet in a fury. Was this really Dr Charles Darlick?

He didn't look like the evil robotics genius Connor had imagined. More like a toddler in a tantrum. Except he wasn't a toddler. He was a little old man with tweedy clothes and blinking short-sighted eyes and hair combed over his bald patch. He looked about as harmless as a pet hamster.

'Are you Dr Darlick?' asked Connor.

'Of course!' spluttered Dr Darlick, still glaring at Mustella with daggers in his eyes.

Connor shook his head in disbelief. He didn't know how to react. It was hard to take this rather pathetic, childlike figure seriously. He started to say, 'What about my grandad?'

when Mustella, in one fluid movement, came slinking up beside him.

She was staring, with her bright, hypnotic eyes, at Dr Darlick. And she seemed to be taking him very seriously indeed.

'Who is Nanny McFiggins?' asked Mustella.

'Wait a minute,' interrupted Connor. 'Who cares who she is? I want my grandad set free from that bungalow, like NOW! I want that Nurse Bot that's keeping him prisoner shut down!'

'And what about Snail Bot?' Simon chipped in.

But Dr Darlick didn't seem to care what they were saying. Perhaps he didn't even hear them. He was staring at Mustella, just as intensely as she was staring at him.

Connor thought, 'What's going on?'

But Simon guessed that Mustella was up to something. He felt a nervous fluttering in his stomach. He knew that look on his sister's face. That bright, focused, excited look. It was the look she wore when she went out hunting.

'Who is Nanny McFiggins?' squeaked Dr Darlick indignantly, as if he somehow resented Mustella speaking her name. He gave a private little giggle to himself. This ignorant and rather weird-looking girl might not know who Nanny was now. But, soon, the whole world would know about her and worship her memory as much as he did.

'Nanny McFiggins,' said Dr Darlick, drawing himself up to his full height, which was about 5 feet 2 inches, 'was my dear old childhood nanny, tragically now dead. I owe everything to her. She made me what I am today.'

As he said this, he couldn't help glancing sideways at Nanny's photo on the wall. She'd been pleased with him before. But you never knew with Nanny. Her mood could change like the wind and, often, you never knew what you'd done to earn her disapproval. Never even knew why you were being punished. Nervously, he smoothed his hair down over his bald spot, and straightened his tweedy tie.

'Did she believe that rubbish written in there?' said Mustella, jerking her neck towards the book Dr Darlick was jealously cuddling.

'To what rubbish are you referring?' huffed Dr Darlick, his cheeks pink with anger. He wanted to be more rude, more aggressive in defence of Nanny. But there was something about this girl. She made him very uneasy.

There was the scent of danger, even lawlessness, about her. He was sure that she and Nanny would have loathed each other.

Mustella said, 'That bit about there being a wild creature inside every child that must be crushed.'

Dr Darlick's voice lost its indignant edge. He loved talking about his old nanny. He never lost a chance to spread her wisdom to others. And this girl seemed genuinely curious. She might learn something from Nanny's teachings. It seemed to him that she was just the sort of child who would have benefited from Nanny's firm discipline. When he sent a Nurse Bot into every home, to make people do what was good for them, this girl's house would be top of his list.

Connor was jigging about. Why were they wasting time on this stupid conversation? 'My grandad . . .' he began.

But Dr Darlick just talked over him. Didn't even seem to notice him. 'Nanny had very firm views about wildness,' he told Mustella. 'She thought it was a very dangerous thing. That it must be guarded against at all times.'

'Oh yeah?' said Mustella. She was back to her old self, cool and confident and slinky again. She'd felt powerless before, when she was faced with machines. But humans like Dr Darlick and his creepy old nanny who feared wildness – she knew exactly how to deal with them.

'Once,' confessed Dr Darlick, 'Nanny caught me climbing a tree.'

'Gosh,' said Mustella. 'You *were* wild.'

Dr Darlick, who didn't understand sarcasm, nodded his head fervently. 'I scuffed my shoes! I was a naughty, disobedient child. I hadn't yet learned that Nanny knew best. But she soon taught me right from wrong.'

'How did she do that? Did she wallop you?' asked Mustella, who never wasted time being tactful.

'Good heavens, no!' said Dr Darlick, scandalized again. 'Nanny wouldn't do that. She had other ways of correcting me. She made me kneel on dried peas for the whole morning. Or she put biscuits crumbs in my bed – Scottish oatcakes were the scratchiest. Or she laced up my boots too tight.'

Nanny had had so many ingenious little punishments that Dr Darlick was spoiled for choice. He didn't mention being shoved down the coal-hole, in the dark, with the scuttling rats. That still gave him nightmares, even now.

But Simon, who'd been listening in growing outrage, burst out, 'What a cruel, spiteful woman!'

Dr Darlick tore his gaze away from Mustella and turned to look at Simon. 'Cruel?' he said in astonishment. 'Nanny wasn't cruel. I deserved it – I was a wild, unruly child. It was for my own good. It didn't do me any harm.'

'But where were your parents while all this was going on?' demanded Simon.

'They were busy,' said Dr Darlick.

He'd been brought up at Darlick Towers – a gloomy old pile miles from anywhere. His parents left Nanny in sole charge of their only child, while they stayed in London in a luxury penthouse. And, on the rare occasions they came back, little Charles was never allowed to see them alone. Nanny was always with him, always watching and listening.

'Look!' exploded Connor. 'What's all this got to do with my grandad? He's on his own in that bungalow with Nurse Bot! It's an emergency . . .'

'I feel very peculiar,' said Dr Darlick, putting a hand to his head and swaying dizzily.

'Mustella,' said Simon, in a warning voice.

'Are you putting mind pictures into his head?'

Mustella just smiled.

'What about my grandad?' protested Connor.

But both boys might have been invisible. Whatever was going on was between Mustella and Dr Darlick. Their eyes were locked. It was as if no one else in the room existed.

'She's scaring him,' Simon whispered to Connor confidently.

And Connor thought, 'Good.' He shut up for a moment about Grandad and let Mustella get on with her work. He'd had a taste of those scary mind pictures. He knew how effective they were. After a dose of those Dr Darlick would probably do anything they asked him.

But Simon was wrong. Mustella wasn't scaring Dr Darlick. Instead, she was giving him a tiny taste of her own wildness. To show him what he'd been missing.

Dr Darlick reeled. Mustella was awakening feelings inside him that had been strictly forbidden, crushed out of him by Nanny McFiggins when he was just a little boy.

He felt himself rippling through grass, with the sun on his back, all his senses alert. He was bounding now, in graceful arcs, feeling the power in his own body, feeling wild and free and fearless –

Dr Darlick staggered and caught hold of his computer desk, seeming as if he were about to collapse.

And Simon suddenly realized what Mustella was *really* doing. He recognized that excited flush on Dr Darlick's cheeks. Mustella wasn't putting Dr Darlick into a panic. She was sending him the same thrilling mind pictures she sent to her little brother from time to time.

'Switch them off,' begged Simon. 'He can't stand it!'

Mustella hesitated. She was having fun. Showing this extra-pathetic human what it was like, living on the wild side. But even she could see that a man like Dr Darlick, starved of wildness for so long, couldn't take the full force of her telepathic powers. So, with a shrug, she stopped the mind pictures.

But already they seemed to have made some difference. Dr Darlick was slouching. He'd thrust his hands deep into his pockets! That was really daring for him – a really big rebellion.

Then Mustella suggested something much

more radical. 'Burn it!' she hissed in her weasel snarl. Her eyes still held Dr Darlick's fascinated gaze.

Connor felt bewildered, left out of the loop. 'What's going on?' he begged. But everyone ignored him.

Dr Darlick looked dazed.

What had happened to him? He had no idea. But his face was lit up as if he'd just made a life-changing discovery. He knew he should shake off this reckless mood, stand up straight, straighten his tie – Nanny would have made him kneel on peas. But he couldn't, he just couldn't. And, for the first time in his life, he didn't seem to care what Nanny thought.

'Burn it!' urged Mustella again, her wereweasel eyes glittering.

'Burn what?' asked Dr Darlick.

'That book you're holding,' said Mustella. 'You don't need it. You don't need *her*.' Mustella's neck jerked sideways to Nanny McFiggins's photo.

If Dr Darlick could have torn his eyes away from Mustella's at that moment and looked into Nanny's stern, goggly gaze, he might have resisted. Who knows? But he couldn't.

But still he wailed, 'Nanny loved me.'

'Rot,' said Mustella rudely.

'But I loved her!'

'No, you didn't,' said Mustella, still holding his eyes with her own. 'You were terrified of her. She was a cruel tyrant, a bully. Burn it!'

With trembling fingers, half-hypnotized, Dr Darlick scrabbled in his desk drawer. Pulled out a box of matches. Was it really going to happen? After a lifetime of believing that Nanny knew best, was he really going to free himself from her?

He actually struck the match. He held *The Wisdom of Nanny McFiggins* in his other hand. But he didn't put the match to the pages. There was a battle going on in his head. Nanny's iron rule couldn't be shaken off in a moment. Perhaps he could never rid himself of her. Did he even want to? The tiny flame was flickering, burning down. What would he do, without Nanny to depend on?

'Burn it!' Mustella was saying. And part of him wanted to, it really did. But then he heard Nanny's voice in his head. 'Wildness must be crushed. It must be crushed. Nanny knows best.'

Still he hesitated. Would he, wouldn't he? But then the decision was taken right out of his hands. Because Snail Bot came clanking out of a cupboard, where it had been waiting to be repaired. Despite its damaged arm it was looking for snails because that's what Snail Bots do.

Simon's head whipped round as he cried out, 'You snail-murdering fiend!' And the little yellow snail on his head, which had held on so valiantly when Simon was trying to escape the Nurse Bot army, suddenly fell off.

It rolled towards Snail Bot. Simon dived to rescue it.

'Burn it,' snarled Mustella. 'What are you waiting for?' The spluttering flame of Dr Darlick's match had reached his fingers. He felt it scorch his skin, winced in pain and dropped it.

Just as Snail Bot let out an almighty blast of methane gas from its rear end.

The tumbling match ignited the gas like a blazing torch. A jet of fire spurted out, hitting the wall like a flame thrower. And the first thing it consumed was Nanny McFiggins's photo. The glass shattered in the searing heat; the photo blistered, curled, went black. But Nanny's goggly eyes seemed to glare at them through the flames.

'Nanny!' cried Dr Darlick, reaching out his arms.

But now the photo was gone, just ashes in the air. And Snail Bot's fiery farts were burning the wall. The Nurse Bot factory was on fire.

'Run!' yelled Connor.

'My snail!' cried Simon, still scrabbling on the floor as black smoke swirled around them and flames licked greedily along the ceiling.

Whump! A glass flask exploded in the heat. There was sparking everywhere and the smell of burning plastic as a fireball incinerated a computer. It was the computer that Dr Darlick used for checking on Grandad and for refining Nurse Bot's programming. Now no one, not even Dr Darlick, knew what was going on inside the bungalow. And, for the first time since she'd rolled off the assembly line, no human being had any input into Nurse Bot's robot brain.

Snail Bot glowed white hot. *Boom!* A powerful blast from its back end launched the little garden bot like a rocket, and sent it crashing through the ceiling. Simon stared up at the jagged, blackened hole. There was sky up there. Snail Bot had gone through the roof. Simon could see it, trailing a fiery tail like a comet, heading into orbit.

'Hurray!' He started cheering, then choked on smoke. Snail Bot might have been blown sky-high, but down here the fire was taking hold.

'Come on!' Mustella and Connor dragged Simon out of the lab, still protesting, 'My snail!' Where had Dr Darlick disappeared to? But they couldn't wait for him. They had to save themselves.

'What about Scooter?' said Connor. 'We can't leave Scooter!'

'Come on! We've got to get out of here!'

Back in Dr Darlick's lab the fire had become a roaring monster. There were loads of inflammable chemicals for it to feed on. Smoke was already seeping out under the door and a grey haze was drifting towards the Nurse Bot assembly line. Soon the flames would follow.

'This way!' said Mustella. She'd found another door. They stumbled through it, coughing, their eyes stinging from smoke.

They were out in that maze of gloomy corridors again.

'Where now?' said Connor. He was hope-
lessly lost. But, for true Sleeths, dark tunnels
are natural hunting grounds. Mustella's
weasel instincts would find the way out.

'Down here!' She darted off.

Connor and Simon had a hard time keeping up with her as she whisked ahead of them
through the shadows.

'No, not down there!' She swerved into
another corridor. The one she was going to
take had a ghostly white glow at the end of it.
It was the fire, spreading through the factory
with terrible speed, chasing them down the
corridors. Would it cut them off?

Suddenly, Mustella yanked open a door. It
was the door she'd let Connor in by – she'd
found her way back to it. They stumbled out,
coughing and dizzy, and collapsed in the
grass, sucking in great lungfuls of fresh air.

Connor forced his smarting eyes half
open. He saw blue sky spinning over him, and
ashes from the fire swirling down like black
snow. Then he felt something wet and raspy
licking his face. He opened his eyes properly.
'Scooter!'

He flung his arms joyfully round the dog's
neck, gave her a big hug. 'Scooter! How did

you get out?' Then he heard a high-pitched, tinny yap.

'Hey, boy!' It was Robo Dog. He wasn't slobbering all over Connor. He was sitting obediently, waiting for instructions. As well as being the perfect pet, was he the perfect rescue dog? Scooter was too scatty to find her way out by herself. Had Robo Dog guided her back to the bot door?

But Connor didn't have time to wonder about that because, as he scrambled to his feet, he suddenly felt heat hit his face. Reflected flames danced in his eyes. The factory was a blazing inferno.

'My snail,' mourned Simon, picking himself up from the grass, his little pale face screwed up in anguish.

Connor didn't know what to say. He would have liked to find some words of comfort. But they both knew that the little snail could never have moved fast enough to escape those flames.

Someone else *had* escaped, though. 'Dr Darlick!' said Mustella. She'd spotted him, with her alert weasel eyes. The roboticist was crouched in the weeds, his face a mask of horror, watching his life's work in ruins.

'Sorry, Nanny,' he cringed, digging his nails into his palm until they drew blood. Nanny McFiggins's photo was gone, but inside his head he still saw her stern, unforgiving eyes glaring at him. Her lips were pressed tight, unsmiling.

'It's the coal-hole for you!' she seemed to be saying.

He'd tried desperately to save his Nurse Bot army, to make them follow him out of the building. But it was no good. Without his computers to give them orders he was sunk. They'd just stared ahead, with their steely faces as blank as the backs of spoons. In the end he'd had to give up, and flee for his life. The Nurse Bot army had been destroyed. They were just puddles of molten metal.

'Sorry, Nanny,' he said again. Now there would never be a Nurse Bot in every home. The assembly line was a write-off. Even the plans for his robot 'carers', stored on his computers, had gone up in smoke.

'Wait a minute,' thought Dr Darlick. How could he have forgotten? There was one Nurse Bot left, the prototype. All he had to do was get her back. And he could start the whole project over again. It would be worth all the effort, to make Nanny McFiggins smile at him once more.

'All is not lost, Nanny,' said Dr Darlick, scurrying off towards Grandad's bungalow.

Mustella watched him race away, like a frightened deer. She knew her mind pictures hadn't worked. That he'd never be wild and free. Even she, with her true Sleeth powers, couldn't make that much difference. His old nanny had a hold over him that couldn't be broken. Even though he was grown up now; even though she'd been dead and buried for years.

Mustella shook her head sorrowfully. 'Poor, crazy guy,' she said.

Simon stared at her in amazement. He'd never known Mustella feel sympathy for any human.

And even Mustella was asking herself, 'Why did you say that?' Why should she care about Dr Charles Darlick? He was an evil control freak, just like his gruesome old nanny. And, suddenly, Mustella was desperate to transform to her weasel self. She'd been human too long and got herself far too involved in human affairs. She had to get away, get out of her human body. Simon was safe; she'd led him out of the fire.

There was still a grey ash cloud hanging over the wasteland and that acrid bonfire stench. But the fire itself was dying down now, burning itself out, as the building slowly collapsed into a blackened, smoking wreck.

Wasn't she supposed to be watching Connor to make sure he didn't tell? 'Maybe you should trust him,' said a hesitant little voice in her head. But that suggestion was so startling, so radical, she couldn't deal with it at the moment. She'd have to think about it later.

But now her human skin was itching, as if ants were crawling all over it. She squirmed in frantic agitation. She just couldn't bear it a second longer. It felt like her brain was going to explode.

So right there, right then, she transformed. Connor and Simon were staring after Dr Darlick. They weren't looking at her. The first thing they saw was a red streak, bounding away, and the white lab coat she'd been wearing in a heap on the grass.

Simon was instantly thrown into a panic. His lost snail was driven right out of his mind. He thought, 'What's she doing, changing

191

in public like this? What's Connor going to think?' And then he saw that Connor didn't look all that surprised.

His buddy was even saying, 'Bye, Mustella. Thanks for the help.'

'You know!' said Simon. So he hadn't been mistaken when he'd read Mustella's lips, back in the factory. 'You know,' Simon repeated, in an appalled voice. 'You know the Sleeth family secret!'

But Connor didn't seem to think it was all that important. He had more urgent things on his mind.

'Come on,' he said, racing off. 'We've got to get Grandad out of that bungalow. We've got to save him from that freaky metal monster!'

Simon stared after Connor, his mind in chaos. He could still hardly believe it. Connor knew the secret. Mustella had told him. And, if Connor told, the consequences would be terrible, catastrophic –

'What you waiting for?' Connor yelled back at him.

So Simon went stumbling after Connor, with Scooter dancing round him in giddy circles and Robo Dog trundling behind.

Chapter Sixteen

The Toilet Bot tribe had almost reached their destination. They had made swift progress through the sewers. Sometimes scuttling along pipes with their tiny sucker feet. Sometimes letting themselves be swept along on underground rivers of sludge. Sewer rats, their ruby eyes wide with wonderment, saw them bobbing by. The bot tribe glittered, like a treasure chest of silver coins scattered on the waves.

Now they were in the grounds of Buckingham Palace. Their blue eyes gleamed; they chittered excitedly to each other in Toilet Bot language. Their dream was almost in sight.

They flowed across the clipped lawn in a shining stream.

'Halt! Who goes there?' A cry came out of

the darkness. Boots crunched towards them. A torch snapped on. Then there was more shouting: 'Nanobot Alert! Nanobot Alert! Condition Red! Scramble the Task Force!'

Searchlights snapped on. Their dazzling beams lit up the bot tribe as if they were on stage. Confused, they stopped and huddled together. This didn't compute; their robot brains couldn't cope. Nothing like this had ever happened down in the safe, cosy world of Grandad's toilet.

Jud, jud, jud, jud.

A deafening throbbing sound came from the sky. There was a great wind that hit the tiny bots with hurricane force. Despite their sucker feet, many were blown away like dried leaves, and smashed to bits against trees and stone statues.

The remaining bots squeezed even closer together. A helicopter was hovering right above them, its rotor blades thumping.

Men in black commando gear, with guns, came swarming down from the copter on ropes. They were members of an elite squad, the Nanobot Protection Task Force, who could respond in minutes to nanobot threats to the royal family. It was well known that such tiny bots were a miniature menace; could even, if allowed to multiply, take over the planet and reduce it to grey goo. And it seemed they were starting with Buckingham Palace!

The Task Force had lots of hi-tech weaponry to blast the bots into oblivion. But they didn't even need their guns. The little bots didn't resist. They weren't programmed to attack or even to defend themselves. They just huddled together while the elite squad simply scrunched them under their big boots, like squashing cockroaches.

It was a terrible mistake; a massive over-reaction – a case of humans and machines misunderstanding each other. The tiny bots weren't dangerous. They weren't even, strictly speaking, nanobots – true nanobots are molecule size. They weren't a threat to the royal family. They were shy, gentle creatures who only meant to serve them.

Down in Grandad's toilet, when they were clustered under the rim, the little machines had chirruped stories to each other. Every tribe has its own myths and stories. And the Toilet Bot myths told of a Great Golden Toilet. It was the dream of every bot to find this toilet paradise, to make it sparkle and gleam.

And where could such a toilet be? The Net gave them some clues. Who would own the Great Golden Toilet, if not the queen? Where would it be, if not Buckingham Palace?

So the little bots had set out to find it.

But now their dream lay in ruins. Their big adventure had met a tragic end. All that was left of the Toilet Bot tribe was mangled metal and wiring, stomped into the dirt. Men searched around in the wreckage to make sure there were no survivors.

Darkness finally fell again on the grounds of Buckingham Palace. The copter whirred into the night, the searchlights were switched off and the soldiers and security guards went away.

Deep among the trees, there was a tiny scrabbling sound. A lone Toilet Bot, blown high up into the branches by the rotor blades, came limping down a tree trunk. Its blue eyes glowed, like pinpricks in the dark.

It was battered, with one leg broken, but it was still functioning. It chittered softly, hoping other Toilet Bots might answer. But there was only silence. It was the last survivor of its tribe.

It dragged itself over the grass, out through the palace railings, and found a drain. *Plop*, it let itself fall through the grille into the scummy water below. And was instantly swept away.

Chapter Seventeen

Connor came crashing through the weeds back to Grandad's bungalow. The security shutters sealed off all the doors and windows like an armoured defence shield. Were they still electrified? Connor wasn't about to touch them to find out.

But then, as he watched, the shutters over the doors and windows began to slide up. Grandad's 'SAVE ME' sign was still taped to the living-room window. But instead of Grandad standing next to it, gazing out, there was Nurse Bot.

Connor's stomach did a sick flip. Had she seen him? He ducked down into the grass. 'What's going on in there?' he raged helplessly. 'What's that metal freak up to now?'

Inside the bungalow, Grandad was wondering the same thing.

He'd just opened his eyes. Amazingly, he felt quite refreshed, like he'd had a good nap. But that couldn't be right. Nurse Bot wouldn't have allowed it. What about toilet trips, taking his medicine or prodding him to see if he'd died yet – all of Nurse Bot's never-ending rules and regulations? And where was his robot 'carer', anyway?

She wasn't in the bedroom with him. It wasn't like her to be so slack, to take her goggly eyes off him, even for a second.

Then Grandad realized something else. There was sunshine coming through his bedroom curtains. Nurse Bot had lifted the security shutters! 'Maybe she's unlocked the doors too,' thought Grandad. 'And I can escape. Maybe she's gone for good.'

But when he hobbled, as fast as his bad knee would let him, into the living room, his hopes were dashed. Nurse Bot was still there. She was standing, with her back to him, staring out into the garden. She even had the window open a little way. What was all that about? Nurse Bot was hardly the type to be charmed by the beauties of nature, or to chill-out and smell the roses. And what was that dreadful music coming out of his stereo?

Singers drooling on about love? How long had that been playing? Grandad shuddered. Where had it come from? He would never sully his jazz collection with that kind of soppy rubbish.

But then he remembered. It was *The World's Most Romantic Love Songs*. He'd got the CD free in a packet of breakfast cereal. He'd probably left it stacked up in his stereo by mistake, along with his jazz CDs. It must have started playing when Nurse Bot put the power back on. That cringe-making, cheesy music was even more reason to get out of here, fast. Grandad hoped, desperately, that the doors would be open.

He thought, 'I'll just slip out now that her back's turned.'

He should have known better. Nurse Bot's bat-like ears picked up his shuffling slippers. She spun round on silent wheels.

Grandad braced himself for her bossy voice, with orders and threats flashing at him in stern red letters from her computer screen: 'TIME FOR TOILET TRIP'; 'NURSE BOT WILL GET CROSS.' But her screen was empty; it just glowed a gentle blue. And what had happened to her face?

Her killer shark glare seemed to have
melted. Those goggly eyes, which could pierce
you like lasers, had a sort of soft, swooning
look in them. Her red rubber lips trembled, in
a coy and hesitant way. But that couldn't be
right. Nurse Bot was never uncertain. Didn't
she always know best?

Something was happening on her chest
screen. Suddenly, there were shooting stars,
hearts and flowers flying all over it. And then,
in sickly pink letters, the words emerged:

I LOVE YOU

Grandad recoiled in disbelief and horror.
'*What?*' Surely his eyes were playing tricks?
Surely there'd been some mistake?

But then came Nurse Bot's voice. Her
Scottish accent was gone. Now she spoke in a
slow American drawl. And her voice, instead
of being strict and bossy, was syrupy sweet.

'I *lurve* you,' she insisted, rolling her eyes.
'You're my kinda guy. We were meant for
each other. Our love was made to last.'

'*Aaargh!*' Grandad backed off. She'd been
scary before. But now she was terrifying!

When Dr Darlick's computers went down,

a big void was left in Nurse Bot's robot brain. It had searched frantically for input, from *anywhere*. At just the same time, *The World's Most Romantic Love Songs* began playing on the stereo. And, since it was the only incoming information, Nurse Bot had simply assimilated it. The sugar-coated lyrics of a CD of slushy love songs were now her new programming.

But Grandad didn't know about all that technical stuff. All he knew was that Nurse seemed to be getting all lovey-dovey. 'This can't be happening,' he thought.

'You're my Mr Wonderful,' gurgled Nurse Bot, gliding closer. She waggled her bristly eyebrows up and down

'Your kisses thrill me.' She puckered up her red rubber lips. Then lunged forward, so all Grandad could see were two eyeballs, wobbling about on their springs.

'Somebody save me!' screamed Grandad, cowering into a corner.

Through the partly open window, Connor heard Grandad's cry for help. He sprang up from his hiding place. 'I'm coming, Grandad!' He was going into that bungalow and nothing, not even Nurse Bot, could stop him.

Connor charged the front door. But it was

already open. He went flying through with Simon, Scooter and Robo Dog close behind. As he skidded into the living room, he saw Nurse Bot. She had Grandad in her grip, her metal arms wrapped round him, her talons gleaming.

Connor threw himself at her. 'Let my grandad go, you monster!' *Clang, clang* went his fists as he furiously pounded her metal body. Suddenly, he fell back, panting, bewildered.

Why was Nurse Bot speaking in an American accent? And what was she saying to Grandad. Was it, 'I will always love you'?

'Eh?' thought Connor.

Suddenly, Grandad's voice rang out, loud and clear. And it said something quite astonishing. 'I don't love you,' Grandad told Nurse Bot. 'I don't love you! Go away. I never ever want to see you again, you metal freak!'

Whirrr. Nurse Bot's circuits hummed, as if they were digesting this new information.

Then her arms slumped to her sides. She said nothing. But two words appeared on her screen. The words were: 'BROKEN-HEARTED.'

She spun round and began gliding out of the room. Simon dodged out of her way.

Scooter dived behind the sofa. But they didn't need to. Nurse Bot simply didn't notice them, even though they were intruders.

There was an expression on her grotesque half-human, half-robot face that Connor couldn't interpret. But Dr Darlick could. He'd just come scuttling in the door. And he stared at his creation, astonished. She looked so lonely, so sad and rejected. All the emotions he'd felt as a child, and still felt now. How could her face show those? He hadn't programmed them in!

Nurse Bot stopped before him. *Whirr* went her robot brain. And then words came out of her mouth.

'I *lurve* you,' she told Dr Darlick, in a voice that was hesitant, but hopeful.

Dr Darlick stared at her. That wasn't one of the things she was supposed to say. He hadn't programmed that in either. It wasn't one of Nanny McFiggins's pearls of wisdom. She would never have said that; he'd never heard the word 'love' pass her lips. It threw him into confusion, hearing those words come out of a face that looked so much like his old nanny's.

Then Nurse Bot did something else that his

old nanny would never have done. She held out a hand, not to slap him, or pinch him or pull his hair. 'Put your little hand in mine,' she said.

Slowly, Dr Darlick rested his soft, human hand in those silver talons, as if he'd found something he'd always, in his heart of hearts, been searching for, but hadn't realized until now. 'Come on, Nurse Bot,' he said.

And they went off like that, hand in hand, out of the bungalow, Nurse Bot gliding and the tiny gnome-like figure of Dr Darlick scurrying beside her.

As they went, Dr Darlick took a green and red book out of his jacket pocket, and dropped it into the weeds. 'I don't need you any more, Nanny McFiggins,' he said, under his breath.

And, for the first time in fifty years, those cruel, critical eyes inside his head, which had censored his every thought and action, were extinguished, like searchlights snapping off.

Words appeared on Nurse Bot's screen. They were in tiny letters, shoved up in one corner. They said:

THE POWER OF LOVE.

Connor stared after the pair until the jungly wasteland swallowed them up. 'That's just *too* weird,' he said, shaking his head. 'I don't even want to *think* about it.'

'That Nurse Bot was a bit fickle,' complained Grandad. 'One minute, she's saying she loves me. And the next she goes off with some other guy! Who was he, by the way?'

'Grandad!' said Connor, appalled. 'For heaven's sake! You're not *jealous*, are you? She was a monster! She made your life a misery! You're not telling me you actually *fancied* her, are you?'

Grandad shook himself back to his senses. 'Of course not!' he said indignantly. 'I'm not that desperate! I just felt sorry for her, that's all. Did you see her face when I told her to go away? I mean, she'd changed from what she was like before. She'd become, well, almost human.'

'She wasn't human, Grandad,' Connor reminded him. 'She was a robot.'

'I know that,' nodded Grandad.

'And that guy she went off with, that was Dr Charles Darlick, the guy who invented her,' explained Connor.

'Yeah, he was a real weirdo,' said Simon.

'As freaky as she was. And he had this evil old nanny . . .'

But Grandad was hardly listening. He was still gazing at the spot in the wasteland where the unlikely pair had disappeared. It sounded strange, but he just had to say it. 'You know, they seem made for each other,' he murmured.

Suddenly, there was a howl from the bathroom.

'Scooter!' said Grandad.

Before they could get to the bathroom, Scooter came dashing out and hid behind the sofa, shivering.

'She's been drinking out of the toilet bowl again,' said Connor.

'But what's scared her?' said Grandad. 'There are no Toilet Bots in there any more.'

Connor went dashing into the bathroom to have a look. And saw Robo Dog, his metal paws up on the toilet rim and his head stuck down the bowl.

'Bad dog!' said Connor. 'Don't copy Scooter! You're supposed to be teaching *her* how to behave.'

Robo Dog didn't look the slightest bit guilty at being told off. He leapt up at Connor, crazy with excitement, his little red eyes flashing. 'Get down!' said Connor. 'Bad dog! Sit down over there!'

Robo Dog didn't obey. Instead, he spun round in circles, chasing his own tail. Then hared into the living room on creaky metal legs, yapping hysterically. How long could his batteries keep going? Surely he'd soon need a recharge?

'I think Scooter's having a very bad influence on that robot,' said Connor, shaking his head sadly.

But Grandad was staring at something in the toilet bowl. Simon had a peek too.

'Something's moving down there,' said Simon.

'It's a Toilet Bot!' cried Grandad joyfully. 'They've come back!' He'd really missed the cheery little cleaners.

'But there's only one,' said Connor. 'What's happened to all the rest?' They had no way of knowing about the Toilet Bots' big adventure. How their modest dream had been wrecked. How they'd been massacred by the Nanobot Protection Task Force.

Now there was only one of them left. It had only just arrived, after navigating its way through sewers back to Grandad's toilet. And it wasn't ever going to leave again. The big wide world was far too dangerous for Toilet Bots. It was going to stay put, where it was safe.

'*Aww*,' said Connor, who, like Grandad, had a soft spot for the little bots. 'It looks sad, all on its own.' Its blue eyes were dim and its cheery little cleaning song subdued.

But not for long. The little bot, on its journey back, had scrabbled under the smoking rubble of the Nurse Bot factory. It had found all the materials it needed to replicate itself. They were stored now, under the toilet rim. Tonight, when it could take a rest from cleaning, it would make itself some companions. The Toilet Bot tribe would be reborn.

'Where are you going, Grandad?' asked Connor as Grandad shuffled off. He chased after him, protectively.

Grandad stood in his open doorway, gazing out at his garden, taking deep breaths of fresh, flowery air. 'It's good to get my independence back,' he said.

'But what about someone to look after you,' fretted Connor. 'I mean, I know Nurse Bot was, like, the carer from *hell*, but you shouldn't be on your own.'

'I'm not on my own,' said Grandad. 'I've got them.' He pointed to Scooter and Robo Dog, playing chasing games out in the wilderness and barking like mad. 'And I've got you. You're always there when I need you.'

Connor swelled with pride. At last, someone was taking his offer to help seriously. But there was one worry, still stalking him like a bogeyman.

'But what if . . .?' he said. 'What if . . .?' He couldn't put his fears into words.

'Look,' said Grandad, reading Connor's mind, 'I'm not going to die. Right? I mean, one day I am. But not any time soon. I survived Nurse Bot. Right? I can survive anything!'

'Have you taken your medicine?' It was on the tip of Connor's tongue to say it. But he stopped himself, just in time. Grandad had just got rid of Nurse Bot. He didn't want anyone else bossing him around.

'So, what are you going to do now, Grandad?' asked Connor.

'What do you mean?'

'Well, you can't stay here, can you?'

'Why not?' said Grandad. 'I like it here. It's like being in the countryside – quiet and peaceful, with no nosy neighbours. I'm staying, so long as that Dr Darlick guy doesn't chuck me out. And something tells me he won't bother. Something tells me he's lost interest in this place.'

'So you're going to keep Scooter here, with Robo Dog?' asked Connor, trying not to sound relieved. He'd never told Grandad how much Scooter got on Mum's nerves.

'Why not?' said Grandad, defiantly. 'Who's to stop me?'

Connor grinned. Grandad was his bolshy old self again. He'd got his fighting spirit back.

'And besides,' Grandad was saying, watching Scooter and Robo Dog playing together, 'I can't part them. It looks to me like they're good mates.'

Connor saw Simon wandering down the garden path. 'Where are you going?' he called after him.

'To get my present from Dad and Mustella,' said Simon. 'Today *is* my birthday, remember?'

Chapter Eighteen

Connor and Simon were sitting inside the caravan, waiting for Mr Sleeth to come back from his rabbit-catching job.

The caravan was a strange, pongy, claustrophobic little den, lined with fur. But, somehow, Connor felt at home in it. It was even quite cosy.

'It hasn't been much of a birthday for you so far, has it?' said Connor. 'Getting caught in that fire, then losing your favourite snail.' He was only trying to make polite conversation. It was getting embarrassing. He and his buddy were sitting in total silence. And Simon was staring at him, just staring, with shocked, disbelieving eyes.

But, suddenly, Simon did speak. Words exploded from him, as if he couldn't hold them in any longer. 'You know the secret, don't you?'

Connor nodded.

'She should never have told you!' said
Simon. He still couldn't understand it.
Mustella was the last person he'd ever have
suspected of letting the secret slip. If anyone
could have weakened, he'd always thought it
would have been him.

Connor steeled himself for Simon's anger.
He expected to be yelled at, threatened:
'Don't you dare tell anyone! Don't you *ever*
breathe a word!' But, to Connor's amazement, what Simon actually said was, 'I'm
really glad you know.'

For Simon, years of loneliness, of not being
able to make a friend, were over. At last Snail
Boy was coming out of his shell.

And words, lots of words, that had been
locked inside him for so long, came tumbling
out of his mouth – all his troubled thoughts.
It was such a luxury, being able to talk to
someone about his divided loyalties, how he
was torn between his mum and his dad and
sister.

'My mum, she thinks it's a curse but my
dad, he says it's special and sometimes I wish
I was special too like them and sometimes I
think, no way, I'm better off like I am, living

with Mum. But then I just think why can't we all get over it and live together? I mean, it's no big deal is it? Being a wereweasel? It's just your genes! Like some people can waggle their ears and some can't.'

'Actually,' admitted Connor, 'I think it's a bigger deal than that – you know, than being able to waggle your ears.'

'Well, maybe I chose a bad example,' began Simon, all prepared to plunge again into the many problems and mysteries of having wereweasel relatives.

But then Simon noticed that Connor wasn't paying attention. That he had a look of stunned surprise on his face and seemed to be concentrating on something going on inside his head.

'Mustella!' thought Simon. 'She's sending him mind pictures.'

Simon was right. Inside Connor's mind, alarming things were happening. Mustella wasn't sending Connor scary pictures – she knew he could block those. And, besides, she didn't want to. Instead, she was giving him a special, privileged glimpse into her private, weasel world. On a roller-coaster mental trip, Connor saw chestnut fur glistening in dark tunnels, smelt fresh rabbit blood and strong musty weasel scent, heard the high, trilling cries of a hunting weasel wriggling through the grass like an eel . . .

'*Phew!*' Connor shook himself like a dog coming out of water. He wasn't sure whether he'd enjoyed that or not. It was awful, exciting, savage, compelling. But, anyway, the pictures had stopped.

Simon looked at him strangely. He said, 'She must like you.'

'Really?' said Connor. He felt oddly flattered. 'Look,' he assured Simon suddenly. 'I'll never tell. Honest. I'll never tell your secret. Cross my heart and hope to die. I *promise.*'

'You don't have to keep going on about it,' said a voice in the doorway. 'I believe you.'

It was Mustella, in human form, dressed in the clothes she'd left outside the factory. She was surprised that she'd just said, 'I believe you.' That she'd overcome her prejudice against humans and found one, besides Simon, she didn't think was pathetic. One she'd decided to trust. She'd never thought that would happen.

She came darting into the caravan, full of her usual restless energy, her eyes bright. She poked her head into a couple of cupboards – nothing interesting there.

Then she pounced at a parcel on the shelf. 'Here,' she said to Simon. 'Happy birthday, bro!'

'Gosh, thanks,' said Simon, unwrapping the rabbit-bone flute and tootling a few notes. A bone flute wasn't much. Not compared with the money and stack of computer games he'd got from Mum this morning. But it was the thought that counted.

'Did Dad make it?' asked Simon.

'Course,' said Mustella. 'He'll be back in a minute.'

'By the way,' Simon warned Connor. 'Don't tell Dad you know the secret. It's just between us three. Right?'

Connor just nodded. He didn't need to start his 'I promise' routine all over again. They trusted him. That was enough.

Then Mustella really amazed him. 'When Dad and me go, when we're travelling around, we could keep in touch.'

'I can't do mind pictures,' Connor reminded her.

'I was thinking about text messages,' said Mustella.

At the same time, she gave a secret grin. She might slip him a mind picture now and again. Just to spice up his boring, normal life when he was sitting in a maths lesson, or taking a SATS exam.

'Hey!' Connor had seen something slide out from behind the tongue of Simon's trainer. It climbed, wobbling, up his sock.

'Your snail!' he cried to Simon. 'It survived.'

'I can't belicve it.' Tenderly, Simon detached the tiny yellow creature from his sock. He cradled it in the palm of his hand. He'd just been thinking about letting all his snails go. He didn't need them any more, not as companions or confidants, now he had Connor to talk to. But he had to keep this one. This one was his lucky snail.

He nestled it snugly in his hair, where it sat, its antennae waving, King of the World.

Mustella raised her eyebrows at Connor. Her glance seemed to say, 'My brother's a bit weird, isn't he?' Which, coming from a wereweasel, was a bit rich.

But Simon was still revelling in his

new-found freedom of speech. He just couldn't stop rabbiting on. 'This is my best birthday ever,' he was saying.

'Really?' said Connor, amazed. It wasn't his idea of a good time, being mobbed by a Nurse Bot army, then almost getting burned to a cinder.

'I'm talking about presents,' explained Simon. 'I got money and lots of other stuff and the flute and my snail back. And something I wished for last night – that Snail Bot, in little bits.'

His whole wish hadn't been granted. He hadn't got the bot's mangled body in a gift-wrapped box. But that didn't matter because the murdering little machine had been blasted into space. Now snails could sleep easy in their shells.

Or, at least, that's what Simon believed.

But his enemy wasn't in bits. It wasn't even a write-off. It was whizzing round the planet, in a sea of other space junk. Gradually, gravity would pull it closer and closer. Would the little bot burn up on re-entry? Who knows? It had already survived flaming farts . . .

So, if you happen to be gazing out of your

bedroom window one cloudless night and see a bright light, blazing its way through the heavens, don't bother to make a wish. Because it might not be a shooting star. It might just be Snail Bot, hurtling back to earth to carry on snail crunching.

Talking about snails had reminded Connor of something. He shifted uncomfortably on the furry seat. He had something to do. Something every boy would do for his buddy. He had to put Simon in the picture about the facts of life. Warn him that if you've learned all you know about sex from snails, you're in for some nasty surprises.

'But not today,' thought Connor. He just couldn't face it today. Anyway, it wasn't the right time. Simon had already had enough shocks on his birthday.

'I'll tell him tomorrow,' decided Connor. 'Or, maybe, the day after.'